Mary,

JADED: LUKE

Laurel Creek Series

I miss you &
Love You

USA *Today* Bestselling Author

HILDIE
McQUEEN

Mother Mary
hope you enjoy
the book
Love Gabe

Jaded: Luke

USA Today Bestselling Author
Hildie McQueen

Pink Door Publishing

Editor: Dark Dreams Editing

Copyright © Hildie McQueen 2017

CHAPTER ONE

T HERE WERE FEW things that scared Luke Hamilton shitless, even fewer the times anyone had intimidated him. At six foot, four and two hundred and twenty pounds of solid muscle, he couldn't remember the last time he'd felt nervous.

Of course, it didn't hurt that there was little he gave a shit about most days.

However, the situation at the moment was a bit unsettling. The coolness of a gun's muzzle at his temple didn't exactly give him a warm fuzzy.

"Give me your wallet," the gravely voice, combined with the stale breath of someone who'd not owned a toothbrush in possibly years, made his blood run icy.

Luke's control was tenuous at best on a regular basis, now with the situation at hand, the hold was quickly unraveling. If this idiot didn't move away soon, Luke wasn't sure he could stop from killing the bastard.

Too consumed with getting his next fix, the gunman let out a low growl. "What you waiting for? Have a death wish? Give me your damn wallet."

The surroundings slowly turned to tones of grey and black, all sound except his heartbeat vanished, and his hands curled into fists.

And now fear decided to make an appearance along with his buddy, the shakes.

"I'm warning you, get away from me." Luke's voice sounded detached and calm, almost as if he'd asked the time or the weather.

The first sign shit was about to get bad.

"SIR, PUT YOUR hands behind your back." The officer, although polite, ensured to keep his distance.

Somehow he had to get control. Every movement he made, even taking shallow breaths, sent spikes of alarm to his unsettled brain. Luke pushed away from the wall of the dimly lit gas station, shaking so hard he could barely remain standing. Good luck on doing whatever it was the police office instructed.

"I'm a war vet. Got PTSD. Give me a second."

The chill in the air combined with his sweat drenched t-shirt didn't help Luke regain control and his teeth chattered. Yeah, the whole junkie vibe didn't help his chances of getting the police officer to believe him.

"Put your hands behind your back now." The order this time was harsher, and Luke prayed the man would not keep pushing and send him back to shitsville.

Measured footsteps crunched on the gravel and he

caught a glimpse of a second pair of black service shoes moving closer. Luke looked up as an older officer joined the first. The familiar eyes met his for an instant.

"What the hell did you do now?"

The first officer didn't lower his gun. "You know him? He about beat a guy to death. Poor sap is on his way to the ER."

Detective Johnson, who Luke had met at the local watering hole, came closer but stopped a couple feet away, giving Luke enough room not to feel crowded. The detective's concerned gaze moved from his bleeding knuckles to Luke's face. "You gotta do something. I thought you agreed to get counseling."

"I did. I went to the VA. They didn't do much more than throw pills at me." Luke turned to the other officer. "I'll get in the back of the car, but no handcuffs."

"Can't let you do that," the officer replied without hesitating. "Against policy. You're under arrest."

Luke knew the rules. Not the first time this had happened. Finally he let out a breath and lowered his shoulders. "Okay."

"I'll do it," Johnson said over his shoulder to the other officer.

Understanding how fragile Luke's hold on reality was, Johnson talked to him the entire time as he handcuffed his wrists behind his back. The words sunk in as Luke worked on regulating his breathing in hopes his body would follow suit.

"Thought you had family in Montana. Open country

may be what you need. Nothing will get rid of the mess in your head Luke, but you have to do something before you end up killing somebody or…" He left off the rest. Johnson didn't have to say anything more.

There was always the permanent way out. There was only one guaranteed way not to have to deal with the fucking episodes that hammered at him constantly.

THE LONG DRIVE to Montana from the Dallas-Fort Worth area would take at least three days. There wasn't any hurry, not like anyone even knew he was headed there.

His family would welcome him home with no hesitation. Behind his back, they'd exchange questioning glances. His mother would fret wondering how long before he left again to not return for another ten years. Much like the old saying, "there's no place like home", it was true in this case.

His home was the only stable thing in his life. And also a stark reminder of how much he'd changed.

Luke appeared and disappeared when he felt like it. No need to explain where he was or what he did. His twin brother had made him promise to always keep the same phone number and answer when he called. The calls were infrequent, but often enough for his brother to know he was alive and not in some sort of state institution or something.

About every three months or so Tobias would call, their conversations lasting just a few minutes, enough for his twin to be assured and in turn ensure their parents were informed of his well-being and whereabouts.

So yeah, he had major issues. Hell, didn't most people have ghosts that came back to haunt them? So maybe the ghosts that disturbed normal folks were nothing like those Luke battled almost daily. Hell, his were more in the classification of demons. Fuckers rarely left him alone long enough to catch a break lately.

Even with music and the windows down, just after Fort Collins, he could barely keep his eyes open. For the past couple of hours, his stomach had been groaning and growling. He supposed the nuts and jerky, he'd eaten hours earlier, were not enough sustenance.

When the truck sputtered Luke glanced at the gas gauge and his brows flew up. "Damn it. Don't cut off on me now." He patted the dashboard and let out a breath when spotting an exit ahead.

He pulled off the interstate and thankfully there was a lone gas station on the right.

While filling up he glanced around noting there was very little around. The interior of the gas station had meager offerings. The last thing he wanted at the moment was more prepackaged crap.

So he paid for the gas, climbed back into his truck and cranked the engine. He turned away from the interstate onto a two-lane road. With the sun below the horizon, there was barely giving enough light to see the surroundings.

Just a couple miles later the perfect combination of a dingy motel and diner came into view. Once he reserved a room, he went straight towards the neon lights that spilled out over the blacktop. A greasy burger, some fries, and a beer would be a good way to end the day.

Other than an older couple, who no doubt drove the dilapidated RV parked across three parking spaces, the diner was empty.

When the bell over the door dinged, a thin pretty-enough woman, who stood at the counter, looked up. Her eyes widened just enough to let him know she was interested.

Sex would be good.

Luke settled into a tall chair at the long barely clean counter ignoring the older couple that craned their necks to look at him.

In their mind, he was either going to rob the place or shoot them. What was it about older people that they always suspected he'd do something stupid? Then again…

"Nice tattoo." The girl who'd moved to stand behind the counter looked at the upper arm tattoo that peeked from under the short sleeve of his t-shirt and then lifted her gaze to his. "Good work."

"Thanks." Luke ensured to look from her face to her chest giving the illusion he was actually admiring the view.

Judging by the lack of luster in her hair and skin, it was clear as day, she was as dead on the inside as he was.

With an empty gaze, from either working too many hours or a hard life, she tapped her pencil to the top of her pad. "Beer?"

"Got anything stronger?"

"Jack."

"That works. Also a burger and fries."

"Got it." She attempted a smile before turning and walking to peer though an opening to where he assumed was the kitchen. She lifted to her toes and called out the order.

With her ass poked out in his direction she looked over her shoulder at him. "On the rocks or straight up?"

Two shots of Jack and a full belly later, Luke honestly didn't care if he got laid or not. Claiming her shift had ended, Jenny, Tami or whatever her name was, sat next to him, perched on a stool, her left hand sliding up and down his inner thigh.

Okay that woke little Luke up, and he grunted while shifting in the chair.

"Want some company?" She leaned closer and pressed her lips against his. She tasted of Jack and mint gum. "Let's have some fun before you get back on the road."

She slid another shot in front of him and poured one

for herself from the bottle she'd brought from behind the counter.

Luke nodded knowing she'd not ask any questions. Hell, she'd not even asked his name yet.

They slammed the shots down and headed to the motel next door.

As soon as they got into the room she lowered to her knees and began unzipping his pants. "Want me to blow you good?"

"Sure." He watched as she took him into her mouth and began sucking with enthusiasm, while her hands worked his length. Obviously experienced, she was good and didn't waste time, seeming to know exactly what it took to bring him close to finishing within a few minutes. His eyes practically rolled back by the time she slid his dick out of her mouth and stood.

"Damn you're hung." She tugged at her jeans, dragging them down without preamble and then pulled her t-shirt off over her head. Jenny or Terry, wasn't wearing a bra. Not at all abashed, she sat on the bed, legs dangling over the side. "Your turn. Take your clothes off."

He didn't waste time and undressed, ensuring to put his pants on a chair on the other side of the bed. After taking a condom out of his wallet, he leaned over and kissed her while stuffing his wallet under the mattress.

There wasn't much cash in the thing, but he needed his identification. One never knew with women like Amy or Terry.

Impatient, she took the condom from his hand and

bit down, tearing the wrapping open. With swift movements, she sheathed him and peered up at him her eyes bright. "There, now get to work."

She spread her legs and Luke obliged.

It wasn't anything close to lovemaking, but more of a race to finish. Ensuring she was satisfied he fucked her until he finally lay spent on the bed with her sprawled over his chest. Interesting that the woman felt comfortable enough to fall asleep, her soft breaths fanning across his chest as he too allowed sleep to take him.

IT WAS STILL dark the next morning when he slipped out of the motel. Mary or Jenny was still fast asleep on her side, her tussled hair framing her face. The woman was pretty in a no nonsense kind of way. Whatever had brought her to this town was probably the same reason she'd not bothered to ask his name.

Luke didn't feel right leaving without at least some sort of goodbye, so he'd scribbled a quick note wishing her well and thanking her for a great time.

CHAPTER TWO

NOTHING LIKE MONTANA. The open sky and rolling hills made him take a deep breath. Seemed a long time since his lungs felt so full. The wind blew into his truck, the wobbling sound reminding him of a helicopter. It didn't matter he could barely hear the country music blaring from the speakers. In his opinion, the freshness of the clean air was worth it. Not just experiencing the scenery of open land in every direction, but to feel himself surrounded by it all. The wind whipped across Luke's face and his lips curved.

He turned down Five-Mile road, the familiarity of where he grew up filling him with warmth. Laurel Creek, Montana was one of those places that stayed the same. The town, built in the early eighteen hundreds, had been home to the Hamilton's since its beginning.

According to the records, his great-great grandparents had arrived with another family, whose daughter was named Laurel. Hence the town's name. The family picked the area because of its beauty and settled there.

Once houses were built, the family farmed for many years before becoming cattle ranchers.

THE GATE TO the Hamilton lands was rarely closed and Luke rolled through the wide opening. Apprehension rolled off his shoulders the familiar surroundings already soothing the tension away. Luke scanned through the windshield in case his brother or cousin were out on horseback.

Cattle ranching had been a prosperous business. For a reason he couldn't remember now, he'd bucked against his father's wishes and instead headed off to join the Army. What an idiot. Now he returned with his damn tail between his legs and head all fucked up. If only the younger Luke would have resisted the call to get away. The appeal of what was beyond the small town had intrigued him. He'd gone as far as he could get. Yeah, he got far…too damn far.

The warm air brought the smell of livestock and open land. Every so often the low mooing of cows rang out followed by another.

Home.

IN THE DISTANCE, he spotted a truck rolling over the uneven terrain toward the stables. His brother Tobias, Luke surmised, because the guy always bought the same color vehicle. Every single truck he'd owned was blue.

Luke chuckled knowing his brother would have a fit when he saw his truck was almost the same shade.

Not sure why he'd picked the color, except maybe a blue vehicle reminded him of his brother. For some reason, Tobias had it in his head no one else in the family should have a blue truck. One of those things that made his twin an idiot.

The family home came into view. The sprawling ranch house immediately bringing a settling in his gut and he pulled to a stop. Luke closed his eyes and let out a long breath.

So far, so good.

His parents had moved out several years earlier deciding to spend their winters in Florida and summers in a nearby town where they'd purchased a small cottage.

Now the ranch house, with its six bedrooms, four bathrooms, and huge open floor plan that included kitchen, dining and living rooms housed only his brother and cousin Taylor.

"Well look what the cat coughed up," his cousin Taylor called out when Luke pulled up to the house. His cousin stood, arms relaxed at his sides with a lazy lopsided grin splitting his tanned face.

Taylor was almost as tall as Luke, but a bit slimmer. Unlike him, his cousin didn't have to go to the gym to stay in shape. Working a ranch was workout enough.

It would have been preferable to be greeted by his brother. Taylor would take great delight in the situation. The guy never let up, persisting on giving a guy a hard time until getting punched in the gut.

Coming home with one's tail between the legs was not exactly a rewarding experience. Last thing Luke needed was ribbing from Taylor at the moment.

Taylor sobered and his gaze went from Luke's face down his body to the truck. Once the assessment was complete there was a shift in his stance and Taylor's shoulders lowered. Obviously he'd passed some sort of test.

The well-masked trepidation left and his cousin's warm eyes met his. "Hey Luke, good to see you man."

"Shouldn't you be working or something?" Luke refused to let his cousin know how glad he was to see him. "I would have preferred a better looking welcoming committee."

"Who says you're welcome." Taylor went to the truck door and pulled out one of Luke's bags, not bothering to ask if he was staying. Seemed to know it was best not to broach the subject yet.

Two trips each and the move-in was done. So much for what his life's possessions added up to.

Taylor dropped down into a chair. "Ex-wife really cleaned you out huh?

"Ya think? Took the house, the car and even the damn dog." Luke joked, he'd been the one to insist she keep everything.

"Wow. That sucks. At least mine left me the dog."

It didn't worry Luke much. They were all material things. The one thing that bugged him was Christina not telling him sooner she'd fallen out of love, or worse, had grown to not feel safe around him.

So yeah, he'd been gone a lot, first with the military and then afterward working as a contractor for the government. Every year that passed, they'd become more distant. During his third four-month stint in the Middle East, she'd informed him on Skype all his belongings were in storage and she was filing for divorce.

And so for two additional years, he'd trudged forward, spending more time away than in the country. The war brought lots of work, so he was not idle for long. Unfortunately, it also brought death, sadness, and grim memories that would stay in with Luke for the rest of his life.

"You've gotten huge. Become a gym rat?"

"Good way to let off steam. Keep myself from losing it."

Taylor studied him. Although his cousin had not served in the military, he'd had a long career in law enforcement until being forced to retire due to injuries sustained when he'd been on a call to stop a bank robbery. It was a miracle the guy was alive.

"I get ya." Shadows crossed his cousin's gaze, memories that were best kept at bay. "Turns out your arrival is perfect timing. We got a battle to fight here."

"Why is that?"

"Got trouble with the landowners on the north side. The Morgans claim our fencing is over the property line. When we didn't move it, cause who really gives a shit, they now want to sue us."

"What the hell?"

His cousin shook his head. "That's what I say. Morgan's daughter is a total freak. Pretty as all get out, but not very likeable."

"Who?"

"Pat Morgan's daughter. Can you believe it? Remember her, she wore braces and always flirted with you at church?

"Not really."

"The one who used to throw rocks at us when we worked near the fence over by their house?" Taylor persisted.

"The one with the huge gap in her front teeth? Damn, what was her name? I called her Pesky, but that's not it."

"That's the one. Pesky. She grew up to become a looker. But also a crazy person."

"What's her name?"

Taylor scratched his head. "Lisa. Or maybe it's Lulu. Hell I don't know."

The tactic to get him from thinking about the things best left in the shadows worked. Luke was curious as to why the woman would be so insistent on things that had not bothered her family for so long. The fence had been built over fifty years earlier. Both families had often repaired it over the years. Either them personally or someone they'd hired. Never once had any of the Morgans expressed concern over it.

True the fence on the north side was almost a quarter mile into the Morgan land. And part of the fencing was also on Hamilton land to allow equal access to water from a creek. Pat Morgan had never voiced not agreeing with the way it was done. Hell after decades, who gave a crap?

"Why haven't we moved it?"

"At first, Toby gave her the finger. Eventually we decided to get it done, but time got away from us. Then we get this legal notice and Toby got pissed. Says he's not moving it now and that he'll pull some kind of homestead law into it.

"That's ridiculous. We'll move it."

"You know how your brother is once he's set his mind on something."

The guy could be stubborn as the day was long. Luke considered what to do about the issue. He decided it was best to drive over to meet the neighbor and let her know the situation would be remedied without need for any legal action.

"I'll go talk to her, and then I'll deal with Tobias."

"Ha!" Taylor let out a loud bark of laughter. "Good luck with that."

"Got anything to eat?" They went to the kitchen and after digging in the refrigerator and finding it lacking, Luke dialed up the local pizza place.

"No delivery? Unbelievable." He let out a long sigh.

"I'll go get it." Taylor pulled keys from his pocket. "Don't bring up the fence with Toby until I get back. I don't want to miss it."

HALF AN HOUR later his twin strolled in through the back door and stopped midstride at seeing him. "Hey bro." He walked over and hugged him. "It's about time you drag your old ass home."

"I'm only a few minutes older than you," Luke said shaking his head. "You look like shit, so I'm the better looking one now."

They were identical twins, but at the moment, they were easy to tell apart. Tobias was much tanner and his muscular physique different than Luke's. Obviously not needing the workouts to get rid of demons. "Not much sleep the last couple weeks. Lots of shit to deal with."

Toby was usually not one to remain stoic and rarely let the drudgery of everyday life get him down. His somber attitude concerned Luke. "What kind of shit?"

"You know. Cows and all that."

"Cows? You are pissed off at a cow?"

"No. Just tired." His brother went to the refrigerator, opened the door and stared inside. "Damn, there's nothing to eat."

"Noticed y'all still expect it to refill itself. All the food Mama left ran out huh?"

A grin split Toby's face. "Yep. It finally did. She called a couple days ago to remind me to run to the store. But, I forgot."

"Taylor went to get pizza."

"Awesome." Toby grabbed a beer and sat down at the table. Every so often he'd look to the door, as if it would make Taylor appear sooner. "What brings you rolling into town all of a sudden? You staying?"

It would be easy to stay there, work on the ranch and not worry about much. He made enough from his military retirement pay and had enough in savings to not worry.

"For the time being, I need to be here. Not sure for how long. But I'm planning to work. Help out and stuff."

"Taylor tell you about the fence?"

"Yeah. Why are you not moving it?"

"Cause it's stupid. It's gonna cost thousands to get that much fencing done."

"You can afford it."

"You mean we?"

Luke rolled his eyes. "Nope, you. I don't get any money from this ranch."

"Yeah you do."

"What the hell are you talking about?" He didn't wait for a reply. "Tobias, just get the damn fence moved. If she sues us, we could lose more than the cost of paying to have it moved."

"So now it's 'we'."

"I'm moving the fence."

"Like hell you are." Toby got up and closed the distance in two strides until almost nose to nose with him. "Don't think because you're all bulked up, I can't kick your ass." His brother's breath fanned over his face. "And what the hell are you doing with a blue truck?"

"Not fighting with you Tobias. I'm just telling you to move the fucking fence and last I checked, a person can buy any damn color vehicle they want. You don't have exclusive rights to the color blue."

"I'm waiting to see who throws the first punch before walking in with the pizza," Taylor said from the doorway.

Luke turned away from his brother. "That was quick. Why don't they deliver if they're that close?"

"Because the Tori owns the place and hates Toby. She punched him in the face last time he walked into her restaurant."

His brother's jaw flexed and he let out a huff. "I'm not eating her pizza."

"More for us." Taylor placed three large boxes and a bag on the table. "Got wings too."

By the hungry look on Toby's face, it wouldn't be long before he joined them.

CHAPTER THREE

"**Y**OU'RE FIRING ME?" Leah Morgan glared at the ass-kisser sitting next to her father before looking to Pat Morgan, the CEO and owner of Morgan Investments. "Dad. You can't be serious. We are on the verge of gaining two major accounts. You need me."

"I need you gone even more." Her father shook his head and gave her a pointed look. "I have two managers threatening to quit because of you."

She racked her brain trying to figure out who he was referring to and then once again looked to Zack, who watched her with fake compassion etched on his face. "You want my job and have done everything in your power to push me out."

"Hold it Leah, I won't stand for your bullying any-one." Her father turned to Zack. "Give us a minute please."

It was hard not to admire the tall, well built man who stood and looked to her, his lips pressed in a tight line before walking out. She'd dated him for a short time until working together and having a relationship didn't work. There were too many variables to list, but she ended it before it got too serious.

Her father cleared his throat. "I want you to take six months off. You have become too overzealous; micromanaging every step of each project to include portions that are not on your plate to do. Leah, I'm asking you to step away out of concern. You will always have a job here, but not right now."

Stunned, she fell back into the chair. Unable to even think clearly, it was almost impossible to formulate a rebuttal. "If I've done anything, it's because I want to ensure the company succeeds."

"We can't succeed alone honey. We need our team. And it's taken me a long time to build this amazing group of professionals. I'm not going to let your overzealousness tear it apart."

Anger surged. "It's Zack isn't it? He wants my job and influenced you in this."

"I've had several complaints and three people considering resignation. Zack asked that I speak to you, but not to force you to take time off. If anything, at the moment, he is the only one in your corner. Judgmental is not something I ever considered you to be."

In a tailor-made blue suit, with a red tie, her father looked every bit the wealthy executive. She'd always been proud of her handsome father. With silver at his sideburns that gave him a distinguished flair, he remained youthful.

They had been working together for the last ten years. Now she felt adrift, as if her lifeboat, the only thing constant in her life, slipped away.

"You don't want me here?"

Her father stood and rounded his desk, coming to sit next to her. "Of course I do. You will take over this company one day. But I need you to get your head together. I need you to have a life. All you do is work and sleep. There is so much more to life than a job."

Of course he was right. Her best friend Allison had just said these exact words to her the day before when she'd finally convinced Leah to join her for after work drinks. There wasn't much that interested her, or that gave her the sense of accomplishment she got after completing a project.

Each day was a repeat of the last, but that wasn't a bad thing. Not in her mind anyway.

"I need you to stay at the ranch for a while. Oversee what has to be done there. Either bring it up to par or prepare it for sale. The choice is up to you since it's yours now. The house has been empty for ten years. There is much to be done. I trust you with this task. Although not corporate work, it is a huge job that I can't leave to just anyone."

Unsure if he was being honest or wanting her out of his hair, Leah let out a huff. "We can contract someone to do all the work. I can do it from here. I promise Dad, I'll rein it back. Don't push me out. Not now." She let out a breath. "I've been dealing with a property line issue as we speak…"

"You will go to Laurel Creek. You are on a six-month sabbatical. And that's that." He returned to sit at his desk. Pushing a button he spoke into the intercom. "Send Zack and William in."

He looked to Leah. "I'm about to brief senior management on the new division of duties. Please ensure you keep a pleasant attitude."

THROUGH HER WINDSHIELD, Leah studied the front of the building she'd been working in for a decade. Beside her on the seat was a small box with a few things she preferred not to leave at her office.

Her accounts had been split between three people and she'd taken the time to brief each one repeating over and over to call her with any concerns. And now as she sat slumped in the overwarm car, she could only blink away tears that formed. It was impossible to leave the accounts she'd worked on for months, even years, in someone else's hands and expect them to be handled properly.

The entire situation stunk. Leaving her position for six months would set her back years and create a lot of work to bring the situation under control once she returned.

Her brain churned and invited her stomach to join in. Leah swallowed as her eyes welled once again.

This was not an ending, it couldn't be. A dragonfly

drifted near and hovered over the windshield, its' beautiful coloring enhanced by the sun's light.

A part of her wanted to start over. After all Leah had enough experience and contacts to start her own company, independent of her father. There were also other corporations who'd hire her in an instant.

Knowing her well and the directions her thoughts would amble in, her father had warned against doing either. Her lips curved at him knowing exactly what she'd be thinking.

"You can go to one of the competitors, or even start your own company, all up to you of course. However, I hope you don't," he'd stated as she cleared off her desk.

"What the hell am I going to do?" she said out loud and put the car in drive to turn out of the parking space heading to Pollyanna Flowers, Allison's shop.

FRIENDS SINCE HIGH school, the two women couldn't be more different and yet their friendship had endured over the years. Allison was the calm to her storm and Leah helped Allison focus when she preferred to go wherever the wind blew.

Today she needed Allison more than ever. Unsure she could face anyone just then, she started the car and went home instead.

TWO DAYS LATER after crying and refusing to leave her condo, Leah trudged into Pollyana.

The smell of fresh cut flowers called for deep breaths and sent the senses to soften. It was a beautiful shop with bouquets in varying vases and a wall one the left side wholly dedicated to different tea blends.

"Hey girl. Who died?" Allison rushed to her, cutting shears in one hand and a long stem red rose in the other.

"Nobody died." Leah winced at the sulkiness in her voice.

"Well good." Brows furrowed and lips pursed, Allison searched her face. "Is someone in the hospital then?"

Leah rolled her eyes. "No. But I am jobless…sorta." She walked to the back of the shop where Allison had a set of beautifully decorated tables. There was always freshly brewed coffee and hot water for tea. "I think today calls for coffee."

"Whoa, this must be pretty bad. You're drinking the hard stuff." Allison put the flower and shears down on the counter and joined her. "But I think you'll drink tea. Black tea mixed with something to calm your nerves."

"Dad wants me to live at our house in Laurel Creek and get the property ready for ranching again, which I'd have to hire someone to manage, or prepare it for sale. He's leaving the decision up to me."

"Makes sense," Allison replied, stirring honey into her tea. "I can understand why he'd leave that job up to you. It's a huge property. I love it out there. I should come with you."

"What?" Leah wanted to stomp her foot. Why did no one seem to think it was devastating, a crippling blow to her career and ego. "Instead of working at my father's multi-million dollar corporation, earning my way to take over one day, I am being sent away to Laurel fucking Creek!"

Taking her free hand, Allison tugged her to a chair. "Sit down."

She did and her friend sat across from her. Allison's wild auburn curls bounced when she shook her head. "I don't get you sometimes. Why would you ever think your dad would do something to hurt you or your career? If people have complained that you're an over the top, butt head boss of the year, it was your doing."

"What are you talking about? I ensured every single project went off without a hitch. My team was always timely with reports and in their handling of deadlines."

"When was the last time you told them how great they are? When did you allow them to work without having to report to you constantly? Did you ever let them decide what worked best on certain things, or did they have to do what you thought was best? Did you step in and take over when you thought they moved too slowly for your liking? If you hadn't, would they have made the deadline anyway?"

Her throat went dry and the breath stuck until her lungs protested. "You knew about this? Dad talked to you?" Tears sprung to her eyes. Angry hot tears at the betrayal by the two people she loved most. "How could

0

you Allison?"

"Oh shut up. I didn't talk to anyone. I know you. I let you run over me like a lawnmower on crack whenever we work on anything together. Don't mind really, cause you end up doing most of the work. What I do mind is that at the end of every single project, you always say the same thing. "Perfect." Then you wipe your hands and move on. You have never said, "You did good Allison," or "I couldn't have done it without you Allison," or even "thank you." Allison leaned forward, her chin on her right palm. "Yep I bet that's how you do things at the company too. I hit the nail on the head." She raised both hands into the air and swayed side to side. "I am psychic."

"You're psycho, is what you are." Leah lowered her shoulders. "Is that true? I don't show appreciation?"

"Oh you do. In your own way, though. You buy me stuff. You pay for drinks or lunch, when we can get to do it, which is rare by the way."

It didn't make her feel better to know she'd not expressed appreciation or encouragement. When she thought about it, she did say "perfect" at the end of a project, but she'd always been fully aware of her team's great work. Had she ever expressed it?

"I am a horrible person."

"Yep, you are. Now, when are we going to Laurel Creek? That hot guy Taylor still live there?"

"Yes he does, lives with Tobias Hamilton at the ranch."

"Tobias is hunky too."

"He's an ass."

Allison laughed. "You noticed it too? He does have a nice perky butt."

It was impossible to stay angry around Allison. "I was too angry to look at it."

"What happened?" Allison sipped her tea while looking at her over the rim.

"The property line. Their fence is over the line by like a quarter of a mile. He refuses to move it. When I go to sell it, it could become a reason for a buyer to back out." She huffed. "I called and spoke to him twice already, the last time he hung up on me."

"Let me get this right," Allison said, putting her cup down. "You each own hundreds of acres and you are fighting over a section of fence. That's crazy."

"The way you're saying it makes it seem trivial. It's not. If you count the fact the fence goes down a for several miles, that's a lot of property."

"Ah," Allison said, distracted when the bell chimed as customers wandered in. "Don't move. Drink more."

The women who walked in were greeted by a cheerful Allison and maintained a happy chatter. After a while, Leah went to the counter to join in and help when another set of customers walked in.

When Allison had first purchased the shop, Leah had spent many an afternoon helping and ensuring Allison had time to the basics, such as running the register and figuring out the cost of materials, etc. Although her friend was an amazing flower designer, Leah had worried Allison would lose money on the venture.

Instead, Allison was doing well and actually began making a profit the first year in business. At Leah's suggestion, Allison incorporated tea into the shop, which suited her friend's need to flitter from one thing to another.

After the women departed, a man arrived and soon after left with a rose bouquet for his wife. They remained at the counter.

"I think you're right. I have been an over the top asshat," Leah mumbled. "Damn, how did I become such a…"

"Butt-Egg?"

"Thanks, that's better than what I would've said." Both laughed at the creative ways they used butt and ass for years. "Yep, I was an asscake."

Allison came to her and placed her arm around Leah's shoulders. "Leah, you need a break. I think your Dad's request makes sense. The land thing can be the perfect way for you to reassess. Meanwhile to keep your juices flowing, you can fight with the Hamilton's."

"I don't want to fight with them. Our parents have been friends and neighbors for generations. I'll set up a meeting so we can have a mature discussion over the matter."

"There ya go!" Allison yelled. "I'm so coming there for a few days."

"Hilda can cover for me," Allison said referring to

her business partner. "She won't mind."

Whether the move to Laurel was good for her or not, Leah went home to her condo in Billings to pack.

CHAPTER FOUR

"**I**'M NOT GOING. You go." Tobias crossed his arms and stared down at the laptop. An email addressed to them had arrived the night before, from Leah Morgan, asking for a meeting. Four p.m. at the Morgan ranch.

"I can't go," Taylor said as he mimicked Tobias' stance. "Uncle Carl asked me to come and help him finish up the gazebo he's building."

One of their cousins was getting married in a couple of months. Their aunt and uncle were pushing for projects to get done since the wedding was taking place at their large backyard in their home just outside of Billings.

Both looked to Luke, who didn't have an excuse for not going. He grunted and rolled his eyes. "Fine, yeah, whatever. I'll go."

"Don't cuss," Tobias instructed. "She'll run and tell Mom."

"Did you tell Dad about it? Why can't he and Mr. Morgan work it out?" Although he'd said he'd go, now

Luke fought for any excuse not to have to deal with the willful Pesky Morgan. "Just going to warn you. If she raises her voice, I'm leaving."

"Maybe we can give her money and tell her to fuck off," Tobias said. "What a waste of time."

"I could try that. We'll see." Luke looked to Taylor. "Bring back some food from Uncle Carl's. Tell Aunt Patty, I want fried chicken."

LEAH SPREAD THE plans on the wide kitchen counter and looked around the open spaces of the great room and dining area combo. Why had she scheduled the meeting so soon? She wasn't prepared. Arriving just that morning, she'd been surprised all the furniture was still draped and very few kitchen items remained.

The cleaning service had done a great job of dusting and vacuuming the house. They'd also cleaned the bathrooms and ensured cobwebs were removed. It had taken four days before the company called her to say the house was livable.

She'd arrived with two suitcases, a computer, her planner, and coffee maker, only to find there were no cups, plates, or any kind of utensil. So, she'd spent two hours at the nearest store, which was over an hour away, gathering necessary items.

Now it was three-thirty and with coffee brewed and brownies in the oven, she felt as ready as one could without a good plan of action.

Needing fresh air, she went to the front door and stepped out onto the wide porch that ran across the entire front of the house. Although some of the paint was chipped, it remained beautiful. It was the picture-perfect first impression to the graceful home she'd grown up in.

A truck rambled toward the house, and she glanced at her watch. Whoever it was came early. The meeting was not for half an hour.

"Damn it." She looked down at her worn jeans and bare feet. She'd hurriedly pulled on a t-shirt and jeans to cook in and had planned to change before the meeting. Too late now.

The truck stopped and a man surfaced. Over six foot of muscles, tattoos and the look of someone who would snap your neck and spit down your throat emerged slowly and sauntered toward her.

Eyes wide, she took a step back. This was not one of the Hamilton's, at least not one that she remembered. Of course she'd seen Tobias and Taylor in the last couple of weeks. Luke, Tobias' twin, was gone. He lived in Texas, or somewhere south.

"Who are you?" she asked standing just inside the doorway. Eyes trained on the man, Leah held the doorknob so she could close it before he reached the porch.

He stopped in his tracks, giving her a chance to study him. This was not your typical Montana rancher. Instead of a Stetson, he wore a baseball cap. No plaid shirt for this man, instead his form fitting dark t-shirt left no illusions of the muscular body underneath. If it weren't for the flatness in his eyes and the stoic expression, she'd find him utterly gorgeous.

At the moment, however, she'd describe him more of a serial killer than a hunk.

A hunky serial killer.

She moved back and closed the door a bit. "Who are you?"

"Luke. I'm Luke Hamilton. And you're Pesky Morgan."

No one had called her that since...well since middle school. Then it was Luke Hamilton who'd started everyone at school calling her that.

"I hate that nickname. Don't ever call me that again." She relaxed and opened the door wider. "What are you doing here? Where's Tobias, or Taylor? We have a meeting."

His wide shoulders lifted and lowered as his upper lip lifted in what she could only describe as an Elvis snarl. "Neither want to deal with you. So they sent me."

"From where?"

"Hell. I'm the devil." His eyebrows rose, the only hint he was kidding.

Leah blew out an annoyed breath. "Well, come in Lucifer. I have to get brownies out of the oven."

Not waiting for him, she hurried to the oven and pulled out the brownies. It was hard to resist burning her mouth and gobbling one they smelled so good.

When she turned, Luke was at the counter peering

down at the plans.

"You can't be serious." His hazel gaze lifted to hers and she knew her dumbass face flushed red.

"Of course I'm serious. It's a lot of land."

He lifted his right hand and rubbed the nape of his neck. Unfortunately it emphasized his bicep, which bulged. "What do you want?"

Okay now this was not the time to lose her train of thought. Especially since she was not as prepared as she'd hoped. "Please sit down." Leah motioned to the barstool. He glanced at it and remained standing.

Leah blew out a breath. If he wanted to play hard-ball, she was a professional at it.

"All I ask is that you or your brother, or whoever owns the ranch, move the fence. Why is that unreasonable? Surely you guys can afford it."

"The fence has been there for over fifty years. If we don't move it, there isn't a damn thing you can do about it." He looked to the paper. "Does your Dad know about this? Are you doing it because you're pissed at someone, got dumped or something?"

"What the hell are you talking about?" Rage surged and Leah barely held back the f-bombs fighting to be let go. One more stupid comment from Luke and she'd let them loose. "Get the hell out. My lawyers will be in contact."

He didn't move, but looked to the brownies instead. "Don't go getting all pissy Pesky. I asked you a simple question."

"So now you're adding insults? Don't fucking call me that."

Seeming more amused than annoyed, he looked around the room. "I remember this place. Hasn't changed a lot."

Leah rounded the counter and wrapped her hands on his upper arm, annoyed when she couldn't get her fingers all the way around it. She tugged him toward the door. "Get out. I mean it."

"We haven't talked. Don't yell."

"I want you to move the fence. My father sent me here to deal with this. I will do as I see fit. Now are you going to move the damn fence, or should I have a work crew tear it down?"

No matter how hard she pulled, he didn't budge. "The cows will get out if you do that."

"I don't give a shit." Once again she tried to pull him. "Will you get on now?"

"Yeah I'm leaving. I'll get back with you in a couple of days. Maybe you'll cool down by then, get laid or something."

Before she could stop herself, she slapped him hard. Her hand stung and he barely flinched. "How dare you? That was uncalled for. Get the fuck out now!"

Without a word he walked to the still open door. Leah shook with anger and watched as he sauntered to the truck. Not in a hurry, but as if it was the most normal thing to be slapped and kicked out.

"You'll pay for this Luke Hamilton," Leah gritted

out. "Asshole."

"OH MY GOD!" At least Allison was friend enough to be astounded at what Luke had said. "He hasn't changed one bit. So different from his twin."

"Tell me about it. Looks different too."

Over the phone she could hear movement. "I'll be there the day after tomorrow. If he comes over while I'm there, he'll get a piece of my mind."

"There's something very different about him. I barely recognized him. Almost as if he's hardened. I don't know how to explain it. It's like he couldn't care less about anything. I know he was stoic before, but now it's as if he's damaged or something."

"Damaged?"

Leah wasn't sure how to put into words what she felt when Luke had been near her. There was heaviness about him. It was as if he'd done things, bad things, and they lingered in him. "I thought he was a serial killer when he arrived."

"So he's not hot like Tobias? I thought they were identical twins."

Tobias and Luke were easy to tell apart now. "No he's attractive, tattooed, and definitely more muscular. But that's not it. You'll see. Maybe you'll see him when you get here."

"Not sure I want to," Allison replied. "Okay, I'll see you on Saturday." The call ended, and Leah bit into her now cold brownie while considering how she'd handle it if she saw Luke again.

He was intimidating, but after he'd come inside, she'd not felt threatened in any way. Although he'd been crass and said stupid things, it was nothing different than the insults they'd hurled at each other as teenagers.

Things were different now. She'd not allow him to insult her. They were adults and even if he'd not left high school mentally, she had.

The sun splayed light across the wooden flooring through the glass panes in French doors. The doors lead to a side garden, and with her cup of tea and the pan of brownies, she made her way to sit outside. No matter what happened in the next few months, one thing was for sure. She'd not let her father, Zack, or the neighbors stop her from getting this project completed and her corporate career back on track.

Maybe she had lost sight of a few things. And although she expected a lot from people, it was not more than she herself was willing to give. Everyone was not wrong, she wasn't so blind not to see how she'd over done it.

But she wasn't about to be underestimated by anyone. The house project would be completed and taken care of and she'd return to Billings. Surely her father wouldn't balk at her returning prior to six months.

CHAPTER FIVE

H IS MEETING WITH Leah hadn't gone off well. Damn, why had he agreed to go as some sort of intermediary. If anything, he would be better suited as the guy who tortured people, not the one who gave victims hope.

Leaning against the steering wheel, he considered going back and apologizing. He had been way out of line. At this point in his life, he was afraid to go near his mama. The shit that flew out of his pie hole was rarely appropriate for any situation other than bars or around other guys.

"Damn it," he said out loud, his gruff voice the only sound in the truck. Although he was almost to town, he hooked a U-turn and headed back to the Morgan ranch.

Pesky had definitely blossomed since high school. Shit, he'd have to stop thinking of her as Pesky but as Leah instead. The woman was an executive for Morgan Investments, and from what Toby said, she was high up on the food chain. Not because she was the boss' daughter, but based on her own achievements.

A shark is how his brother said she was referred to. One thing was for sure, other than dealing with someone at a bank or some shit like that, he rarely spoke to a woman like her. Although the Leah he'd just spoken to had cussed him out, it seemed out of character for her. Leave it to him to draw the sailor mouth out of even a classy lady.

In worn jeans and bare feet, Leah Morgan still exuded class. Very little remained of the pesky young girl who'd thrown rocks at him as a teenager. He'd made her cry on more than one occasion back then. As if the land issue wasn't a bitch, now he wondered if resentments from the past were one more reason he shouldn't be the one attempting to make peace.

Luck was on his side. Leah was outside looking up at the house when he neared. She turned toward the sound of his truck, shading her eyes with her right hand. Immediately upon seeing him, she spread her feet, placed fists on her hips and glared.

"What do you want? I made it clear you're not welcome here," she called out as he climbed out of the truck. "If you don't get off my property Luke Hamilton, I will call the police."

"Don't do that. Eric will take great pleasure in throwing me in jail." Truth, he and his cousin didn't exactly see eye to eye. "Give me a minute please. That's all I ask."

Although she rolled her eyes and a sneer curled her

lip, it didn't detract from her beauty. If anything, an angry Leah was astonishingly sexy. Damn if his mind didn't dive into the gutter and he pictured her riding him, her mouth swollen by his kisses, his hands covering the small mounds on her chest.

"Hello?" she snapped. "What do you have to say that you're willing to go to jail for?" Cell phone in hand, she lifted it to her ear. "You've got about five seconds."

"I apologize. I was way out of line to say those things. Please accept my apology."

"Hi, yes, is Eric Hamilton around?" she spoke into the phone, her eyes glued on him. "No nothing urgent, I'll call back later. Thanks." She hung up and lifted a brow.

Since she didn't give any indication of accepting his apology, Luke figured he'd better try again. "I'm sure we can work on the fence issue. I'll get it moved. But you have to admit, it's not a battle worth fighting over."

"For the Hamiltons, it's not. You're getting free land for encroaching…"

"We don't encroach. I'm sure it was an honest mistake. A mistake made many years ago. Your father never said anything."

She huffed. "I'm the one who's been put in charge of overseeing the property and deciding what is best. If you are moving the fence, then ensure it's done by the end of the month. Your contractor can meet with my surveyor. I will email the information to Tobias." Leah glanced over him. "Anything else?"

Luke pressed his lips together to keep from telling her to kiss his ass. "Nope."

A gust of wind blew and a flapping noise on the house sounded. She turned back to the house and lifted both hands to shade her eyes. "What the hell is that?"

"Probably loose shingles or a pack of squirrels," Luke mumbled. He'd not heard anything. "See ya."

"Wait." She moved backward still looking up at the house. "Do you know a qualified roofer? Doesn't your uncle own a roofing company?"

"He retired years ago."

"Oh. There's a strange sound coming from the ceiling."

He wasn't about to climb up on a damn roof to ensure the woman wasn't spooked. At the same time, he did want a new start there in Montana. Making amends with a neighbor was probably a good way to begin.

"Got a ladder?"

"You don't have to look."

"I know that." He walked around the side of the house with Leah on his heels and upon seeing a shed, went toward it.

"There's probably snakes and spiders in there." Leah informed him of the obvious. Suddenly Wonder Woman had turned into a scared mess.

The door was locked, so she raced into the house and returned with a set of keys. Once they unlocked the wooden door, he went into the dim interior and found a ladder.

After leaning the ladder on the side of the house, he climbed up and onto the roof. Luke had to pause when turning around and seeing the view from there. Land stretched as far as the eye could see, including the Hamilton lands.

If it weren't for the current situation, he'd lower to his ass and stare into the distance. Luke studied the roof. His boots crunching on the weathered tiles as a crack sounded. Another gust of wind blew and several pieces of roofing flew from where he'd walked.

"Definitely need a new roof," he called down. "The loose shingles is probably the noise you hear."

The roof creaked as he walked in a circle, the ominous sound made him freeze. "Probably need some repair work done. The shit is cracking and creaking under me."

"Get down from there before you fall," Leah called up. "No use in you getting hurt."

Luke took a step and stopped when the roof dipped. He eyed the distance to the edge of the house. A couple of jumps and he could reach the edge where the ladder was. He leaned forward, and just as he was about to jump, the roof gave way.

THROUGH CRACKING OF material and crashing past wood he landed in an empty room with a loud whomp followed by smattering debris falling all over him.

Leah called out his name and he could make out her footfalls as she rushed toward the doorway. Other than a couple of cuts and scrapes, seemed he'd made it all right. He lowered his head back onto the floor and let out a breath. The blue sky was visible through the new opening he'd just made.

"Luke!" Leah rushed toward him just as a thought struck. "Are you all right?"

"Give me a minute to get my breath," he said, puffing each word out. "Not sure but I may have hurt my right hip. Is there something sticking into it?"

She leaned across him and slid her hands over his hip and under it, her body touching his in a most intimate manner. "I don't see anything. Your jeans are torn here." She pressed closed to his crotch. "Is this where it hurts?"

"Yeah, that's it." He was going to hell, but damn if this wasn't pretty close to the picture he'd imagined earlier. "Anything poking me there?

She leaned closer to study the skin. "No. I don't see anything. You're bleeding from a scratch though."

"Okay. That's good." Luke kept his voice low and breathless. "I'll be all right."

He went to sit up, but she pushed him back down. "What if you have a concussion? I don't think you're supposed to get up right away."

"I'm okay."

She placed both hands on each side of his face and stared into his eyes. "Can you see me clearly?"

So maybe a concussion wasn't that bad of a deal. "Not really. You're fuzzy around the edges." He lied again.

"Oh no." She looked up at the ceiling. "I'll call an ambulance."

"How about you just help me to the living room. I'm good. I've survived way worse in Afghanistan."

He sat up and pretended to have trouble standing. She lifted his arm and put it over her shoulder. Luke wanted to laugh. His arm probably weighed more than she did. Nonetheless, her plush body against his as they made their way to the couch was more than enough payment for busting his ass.

Once they fell onto the couch together and she managed to get out from under his arm, she continued studying him. "You sure I shouldn't get you to a doctor?"

"Yeah, I'm good. I'll take a glass of water though."

She returned with the water and instead of sitting next to him lowered to the ottoman. "You don't look anything like you did in high school."

"Neither do you. It's been twenty-five years or so. We've changed." Wasn't that the damn truth.

She let out a long breath. "The sooner I get this all done, the faster I can get back to my life." Her scowl softened as she looked around the interior of her family home. "I'm not sure what to do about this house, or the land. It's up to me whether to keep it or sell it all."

Had she grown so hardened that she'd give up her family lands? No matter how shitty things got for him, the fact that Hamilton lands remained and he could return to them kept him grounded. The ranch was the only thing that stopped him from totally losing his shit and blowing his brains out at times.

"Yeah, well, I better get on my way." He wasn't about to give her any kind of advice. The last thing anyone would want from him was any kind of counseling. If anything, he was more suited as the poster child of what not to do with your life.

Luke placed the glass down next to Leah and stood. "I'll see about that fence." He stalked to the door cringing at the sting from a rather nasty looking scrape on his forearm.

"I feel bad. Do you mind if I run down to the drugstore and pick up some stuff. I can ensure your wounds are cleaned out and bandaged." Her eyes rounded. "Oh my God, you're bleeding a lot here." She pointed to his left side. He'd not noticed the large bloody stain on his torn t-shirt.

What did one more scar matter? "Nah don't worry about it." Without another look at her, he hurried to the truck. Would have to put off his trip to town until the next day. His presence always seemed to make people wary, showing up bloody would probably freak people out.

THE HOUSE WAS empty when he arrived. Remembering both his brother and cousin had errands and work to do, Luke went to the cabinet where all the first aid stuff was kept. Being it was a working ranch, there were always some well-stocked first aid kits around.

He stripped and went to the bathroom. Looking in the mirror, he studied the cuts and abrasions. The worst one was the one on his left side. Seemed something had scraped him on his way down. There were probably splinters and shit in there. Good thing it was fairly shallow, hopefully nothing was punctured other than his skin.

The most painful was the large scrape on his forearm. He lifted his arm to get a better look. Nothing to be done about that one except keep it protected and clean.

He stepped into the shower and hissed at the stinging when the warm water hit his injuries.

CHAPTER SIX

THE CLERK BEHIND the counter, a pleasant plump woman, smiled broadly at her. "Hey stranger, it's been a while since you came to town."

Leah read the woman's nametag. It didn't ring a bell. Someone from high school? A family friend? She got nothing.

"Hello Jean. I am only here for a couple of months. Doing some things at the property."

"It's a shame no one's been living there. It's such a beautiful house." She eyed her purchases. Bandages, antiseptic ointment, peroxide and some Band-Aids. If she used everything on the counter, the man would end up looking like a mummy.

It wasn't just concern that drove her to check on Luke Hamilton, but fear he'd get his wits about him and sue her.

Leah tried to remember if she'd asked him to climb up there or if he'd volunteered. Either way, he'd been harmed on her property and could very well blame any lasting injuries on her.

She remembered the wound on his side. It was bleeding quite a bit and she'd not gotten a chance to see if he'd been cut bad enough to warrant stitches.

All kinds of scenarios rushed through her mind as she ducked into the bakery next door and grabbed half a dozen muffins to bring with her. Her mother had always assured her food and an apology did wonders when it came to men.

Not that she wanted to think about any sort of friendship with a man. Her ex-husband was the perfect deterrent for any kind of romanticizing.

One-night stands, or an occasional hookup were fine. A relationship, no way.

Driving through the tall archway onto the Hamilton's ranch, Leah tried to remember the last time she'd been there. It was in middle school, after her father had caught her throwing rocks at Luke and Toby. It has been the worst day of her fourteen-year-old life. She'd stood next to her dad and apologized while Mrs. Hamilton had assured her everything was okay, stating the boys probably deserved it.

The twins had been gracious and accepted her apology. Luke however had smirked through his acceptance, which made her want to find a rock and smash it into his face.

Thank God the twins were in high school at that point, so he couldn't pick on her at school. Nonetheless, she'd never liked Luke since then. Toby and her had remained amicable whenever she'd returned to town to visit her parents.

Luke had joined the Army by then and was gone until now.

Her phone buzzed and she answered it upon seeing her mother's name pop up.

"Hey Mom."

They spoke about what she was doing there at the ranch, her mother hesitant upon hearing her mention she might decide to sell the land.

"Don't be hasty. That land has been in your father's family for over a century. Why don't you consider a business venture? You're a smart businesswoman."

Deciding it was best to change the subject, Leah cleared her throat. "I'm going to the Hamilton's, just now pulling up to the house. Luke was checking the roof and fell through. I need to make sure he's okay."

"Oh dear. Be careful. His mother told me he's not been the same since coming back from overseas. He might have PTSD or something. Anyway, be sure Toby or Taylor are around before you spend time alone with him."

"He is very different," Leah replied. "I'll be careful. I better go, I'm here. I'll call you later Mom."

She eyed the house. It was a beautiful log home that had been built by Luke's grandfather. Luke's parents had remodeled it, making the beautiful house rustic and graceful at the same time.

When she knocked, there was a deep grumble.

"Coming."

The door open to reveal a shirtless Luke Hamilton. As hard as she tried, Leah couldn't help but take in his muscular physique. A tattoo of what looked to be a raven spread from his right upper arm to his chest. The rest of his torso was not inked, but marked nonetheless. An angry scar ripped across from his left ribcage to his stomach. The same side that was currently bloody.

His flat gaze went from her face to the bag and box she held. "What's up?"

"I came to make sure you were okay. I feel horrible about your fall." She looked past him to the dim interior, wondering if either Toby or Taylor were there. "I brought muffins," Leah finished weakly.

Eyes flitting past her toward the stables, he remained still as a statue.

Just when she thought he'd tell her to leave, Luke took a step backward. "Come in."

The house was not at all like she remembered it. Rich leather couches and weathered farm style furnishings filled the space. Past the main room, she spotted a breathtaking white kitchen. "Wow this place is amazing." Leah grimaced. She sounded like one of those people on television after a home make-over.

"Mom decorated it." Luke held a t-shirt in one hand and seemed to consider what to do next. "Took a shower and cleaned up. Nothing to worry about."

Fresh blood seeped from his side. "I think you might need to see about that cut there." With both hands full, she motioned with the muffin box to his side. "Do you mind if I put these down?"

"Nope." He waved her toward the kitchen and followed her there. The entire time every inch of her body aware of his much larger one so close behind. This was not the time to have a sex fantasy with a bad boy. Leah blew out a breath and placed the muffins on a large island. "You guys keep this place pretty tidy."

Luke looked around as if seeing things for the first time. "Cleaning lady."

"Ah."

"Want a beer?" His manners had kicked in it seemed as he went to the refrigerator and pulled out two beers, not waiting for her reply. He threw the t-shirt over the back of a stool and opened the beers. After sliding one in front of her, he took a long draw from his, the entire time his gaze on her.

"Can I look at that?" She neared and his eyes immediately shot to the discarded t-shirt. Was he afraid of being touched? Somehow she doubted it.

"Yeah sure, but I think it's fine. It'll stop leaking. That's why I haven't put the shirt on, don't want to stain it." He moved backward and looked around as if trying to decide where to sit.

They walked back to the living room. Luke carried the beers and she brought the bag with first aid items. "Where are Toby and Taylor?" Her mother's warning struck, although admittedly, she didn't feel threatened at all by Luke at the moment. If anything, it seemed more as if he was the one unsure of her being there.

"Working."

"Where's the bathroom? I need to wash my hands." After he motioned to a door near the entryway, she went and washed her hands thoroughly.

When she walked back to the living room, he remained sitting, his attention on the bag she'd brought.

"Lay back."

He took another long swig of his beer and fell back on the couch after putting the empty bottle down beside hers on the coffee table.

The display of a gorgeous man with one leg draped over the side of the couch and one arm under his head was enough to make most women drool. Leah pretended to be fascinated by what was in the bag instead. "I'll rinse it out and put antiseptic on it. I'll bandage it, but you should remove it and let the cut air out once the bleeding stops. Probably want to be pretty still until then."

"You sound like a doctor."

A smile curled her lips. "I took a few nursing classes in college. For a bit, I considered going into nursing."

"Changed your mind huh?" He grimaced when she dabbed at the cut with peroxide, which bubbled. Despite him having showered there was still some debris in it.

"I'm going to have to wipe it out. It'll sting." Leah took two bandages and soaked them in saline solution. Trying to distract him, she talked. "Mom said you went overseas. Where did you go?"

"Afghanistan and Iraq."

She expected him to flinch, grunt, or have some reaction to what she knew was very painful. Instead he was steady, his breathing even and his eyes on her. Flustered at his perusal, she considered what to say next.

"What happened?" She pointed to his old scar.

"IED."

"Oh. Sorry, probably shouldn't have brought it up."

"Probably." He looked away to the window. "Look I appreciate this, but you don't have to patch me up. I'll take care of it."

He went to lift up and she pushed his shoulder, the touch seeming to burn them both. Leah's mouth parted as she took a deep breath, and he glowered at her.

"I'm sorry. I'll just put this on here and be on my way."

She quickly placed folded gauze over the wound, and then taped it in place. At least he didn't seem to be particularly interested in her. If anything, Luke looked ready to tell her to leave him the hell alone.

"I better go. I'll leave those here." She motioned to the first aid items.

"Nah, take them. We have plenty around here. You might need them."

While she gathered the items, he continued to watch her. "Get your roof patched. It's supposed to rain." He'd gotten up and within seconds was shrugging on the shirt. As each inch was covered, Leah's gaze followed the fabric's descent.

With her items in hand, Leah walked out the door,

she turned to him. "Let me know about the fence. I need to move on with getting the ranch ready for sale."

"How can you do that? Sell your birthright?"

She gritted her teeth. "I don't live here. My parents don't live here. My brother has no desire to move back. He has settled on his wife's family lands in Wyoming."

Without responding, he looked past her toward the expanse of Hamilton lands. The property much larger than her family's. "Suit yourself." He shrugged and closed the door in her face.

Leah blinked at the closed door, her mouth falling open. Had the asshole really just slammed a door in her face?

That's what she got for trying to be nice. If anything, his actions reinforced it was best to get away from Laurel Creek. The sooner, the better.

CHAPTER SEVEN

LUKE COULD FINALLY allow his breathing to accelerate. It had taken all his will power not to pull Leah down over him. To kiss her senseless until she'd let him fuck her.

Somehow, some sort of reason prevailed and he'd been glad when she left. Otherwise, he would've had to toss her out.

While she'd ministered to his wound, his entire body from head to toe was strung tight as a tripwire. Every inch begged for her attention.

It was stupid to have allowed her to touch him or to remain so close for as long as she did. Not just the soft expensive perfume and glossy hair, but every part of her had enticed him past reason. She was lucky he'd not grabbed her by the hair and pulled her down to take her mouth with his.

The woman affected him.

"Shit." He stalked to the kitchen and looked at the muffin box. A part of him wanted to smash his fist into it, but the growling in his gut reminded him he'd not eaten much since the bologna sandwich he'd made for breakfast.

THE DINGY BAR was exactly the kind of place Luke needed to stay away from. At the same time, the familiarity of stale cigarette smoke and lack of lighting made him feel at home. He sat at a barstool watching two guys argue by the pool tables as another older man, lost in thought, slumped over his beer.

"Another shot?" The bartender, a guy he barely remembered from high school, eyed his empty shot glass and refilled it at Luke's nod.

Something simmered just beneath the surface. Luke hated the feeling that was only relieved by distracting himself. Too wired to remain at the house, he'd come to the desolate drinking hole on the outskirts of town. Yeah, it was a dumb move as he felt the affects of the fourth shot. Although traffic would be light heading home, he'd not chance it by driving.

After slamming the shot down, he tapped the bar. "Gimme another."

He felt her before seeing her, and turned to see the hungry look of a woman more desperate than him. "Don't I know you?"

Fuck no. They both knew it. "Maybe."

She slid onto the stool next to his and giggled while pretending to have trouble settling. He steadied her.

"Can I buy you a drink?"

The woman brightened. "Sure."

Considering he'd probably sleep in his truck, he wondered if he would take the woman up on what she'd offer after a couple more drinks. He needed something, and even if it was a blow job in the bathroom, it would help to take the edge off.

Sure enough, a couple of drinks later, the woman, Sally or Patty, leaned into his ear. "Wanna come over to my place?"

He compared her to the woman whose light touch had sent his body to full alert. The perfume on Patty, or whatever her name was, didn't make him want to inhale deeper like Leah's had.

"I'm flattered, but I better not." He pretended enough interest to allow his gaze to linger over hers.

He was an idiot.

CHAPTER EIGHT

H ER CAR SWAYED this way and that over uneven terrain to the fence line. Leah wondered what in the hell she was thinking not renting a truck or SUV? At this rate, she'd have to take her BMW in for an alignment or new muffler. A loud bump on the undercarriage made her cringe.

"Damn it! I need to be in an office," she said out loud. "This shit sucks."

She spotted two men on horseback and slowed down. It looked like Toby and Luke had mounted and headed to where a crew of men worked on the fence.

Nearby several cows meandered toward the activity, probably the reason why the twins rode toward the fence. Not to oversee the project, but to cut the animals off from going onto her land.

Deciding it was best to walk the rest of the way, she got out of her car. No use in finishing whatever damage she'd done. Just as she got a few yards from her car, Luke waived to get her attention.

"Get back in your car!" Luke screamed. "There's a bull loose."

Leah looked in every direction not seeing anything other than cows. But she didn't need to be told twice. Hoofs sounded and she yelped at spotting an angry bull charging towards her.

Racing to her car although the animal was quite far, she fought to keep from screaming the entire time until safely ensconced within the metal structure.

Luke's horse galloped into the bull's path, rider and horse seeming one as he circled getting the bull's attention. The animal slowed, and seeming to lose steam, turned in its path heading back toward the Hamilton lands.

It was enthralling to watch when Toby took over galloping in circles guiding the bull away without getting too close.

Both men belonged there. Being descendants of cattle ranchers, they'd not lost touch with their heritage.

When rider and horse neared, she got out of the car. He looked down at her, his face shaded by his black Stetson. "The bull got out of his pen. Was chasing after the cows who decided to come investigate the commotion."

Unlike the last time she'd seen him, Luke seemed at ease, friendly almost.

Almost.

The team the Hamilton's hired was smaller than she expected. With only four men, it would take weeks to do the miles of fencing. She shaded her eyes and looked into the distance, not seeing anyone else. "Is this the entire team?"

"Yes. You didn't give us much notice."

At this point, Toby neared. He acknowledged her with a nod before looking to Luke. The twins were identical, but not so much now as Toby wasn't as built or appeared to have any tattoos.

Luke lifted a brow. "You didn't give us a timeline for the project to be finished. Just said it had to be done."

Leah couldn't help letting out a huff. "Seriously? At this rate, it could take a year." Grinding her teeth to keep from cussing, she pinched the space between her eyes. A headache threatened. "This is not acceptable."

His face hardening, Luke dismounted and Toby followed suit. The twins moved forward, but Toby moved faster almost as if to step between where she stood and his brother.

Undaunted by his twin, Luke's flat stare bore into her. "Tough shit. I don't care if it takes two years."

Before he could continue, Toby interrupted. "Look Leah. You come out of nowhere with a demand about something that neither of our families have ever had a problem with. I'm willing to bet if you survey the land over by the creek, the fence is deeper into our land than it should be. I believe our grandfather did that to be fair to yours. They wanted to ensure the cattle had plenty of access to water."

"I've had the entire property line surveyed and that is

not true." She crossed her arms, too angry to keep from tapping her foot. "I won't be bullied by you Hamiltons again."

Luke's eyes narrowed. "Is that what this is all about? What happened when we were young and stupid?"

"No. This is about what's right."

He took a step forward and Toby pushed him back. "Luke go see about the cows. I'll talk to her."

Something transpired between the brothers. Tobias didn't back down, his hand on Luke's shoulder. "Go on."

Finally Luke lowered his shoulders and turned away.

Toby waited until after his brother was out of ear-shot. "Don't provoke him. He's not the same guy from high school."

Her temper, which up to this moment was managed, finally escaped. "I'm not provoking anyone. I'm just asking for what is legally in my right to demand. We're talking about a lot of land."

Tobias looked to the men who'd stopped working and watched with interest. "Patch it up boys, close the gap and call it a day. We're done."

"What the hell are you doing?" Leah looked between the men who continued watching and Toby. "Why are you stopping?"

When Tobias' hazel eyes darkened, they reminded her more of Luke's. The firmness of his jawline and flare of his nostrils made her wonder if Luke was the only twin with anger management issues. "Homestead act of

1910 covers us. I will submit the paperwork proving we've been on this part of Morgan land since 1872 and file for a deed. Now get the fuck off our property."

He turned to the horse, mounted and rode off.

This would definitely not be the last of it. Undeterred by his pronouncement, she stalked to her car intent on beating him to sue for her land back.

"NO, YOU WILL not." Her father's stern tone made Leah wonder if all men somehow communicated through some hidden system. "He's right. Technically the land is theirs. If you go ahead with the sale, which I don't know yet that I approve of, the buyer won't balk over a narrow strip of land. Not when we're talking about over one hundred and fifty acres."

Leah sat up straighter. "What do you mean, you may not approve? You asked that I come here to see about prospering the ranch or seeing what kind of profit can be made by selling it. And, you also said that it was my decision." A harsh breath escaped. "You don't mean to do anything with this ranch do you? It was just a way to push me out."

"I have not changed my stance on the fact you will step into my shoes when I retire. However, you needed to step back and regroup. Right now it seems as if you're not changing one bit." He ended the call and she stared at the display.

The world had gone insane. A tapping on the car

window made her jump and she lowered it.

"Here to see about patching up the roof." An older man looked from her to the roof, as if anxious to get away from her. Probably because she was scowling and glaring at him.

"Yes of course."

ALTHOUGH NOT IN the mood for a social situation, Leah was tired of eating take out and cold cuts. She walked into Melba's, a diner that had always been in Laurel Creek for as long as she could remember. Spotting an empty booth, she hurried to it only to stop when spotting Luke sitting in the one next to it. He looked up, and for a moment it seemed as if neither could look away.

He motioned to the bench opposite him. "Welcome to join me."

It would be awkward now to sit on the one next to his and besides, he wasn't about to scare her off, so she nodded and slid onto the bench. "I didn't want to eat another cold sandwich. What's your excuse?"

"I didn't feel like cooking."

It was hard to picture him cooking, much less doing any kind of domestic chores. But, she supposed he'd have to know how to do for himself since he had to be close to forty-five. "You cook much?"

Luke waited until the waitress took her order after sliding a hamburger and pile of fries in front of him. He motioned for her to refill his soft drink. "Yeah, almost everyday since getting here. Toby and Taylor don't cook much more than what they can nuke."

"I can't picture you cooking." She watched him bite into the hamburger and resisted the urge to reach for one of the French fries.

Seeming to read her mind, he turned the plate sideways and motioned to the potatoes. Since his mouth was full, he didn't say anything.

"You can have some of mine when she brings my burger." Strange as it was, eating from his plate didn't seem awkward at all. Interesting how they seemed to have two different relationships, she and Luke. There was the pseudo friendship from years of knowing each other and the strained interactions over the property.

"I think my Dad is trying to push me out of the family business," she blurted out the words, needing to say them aloud. "Now he's saying I can't sell the ranch."

Luke wiped his mouth, his gaze not meeting hers, instead on his food. "What do you want to do most right now?"

The question was so simple, and yet it caught her by surprise. "I want my life back. I'm a good executive."

"If that's true, why are you here?"

She looked out the window. Why had she not pondered that? Instead of taking time to think, to consider the reasons behind her being sent away for a sabbatical, she'd brewed over it and thrown herself into a property fight over a strip of land that lay between two families who'd coexisted for over half a century.

"I suppose because I've changed. Since my di-vorce..." The server returned with her food and she was grateful. Best to eat and keep from spilling her guts to a guy who didn't give a shit about anything.

CHAPTER NINE

A MYRIAD OF expressions flickered across Leah's face. She didn't realize how expressive she was. Luke wondered if one of the reasons she'd had to leave the corporate world was because others could tell what she thought by her expressions.

He wanted to laugh at the possible misunderstandings that could have occurred.

"Divorce has a way of changing a person."

Of course he wasn't going to go down the "been done wrong" lane with her, but it was the truth. A failed marriage was not something that he considered one of his proudest accomplishments. Divorce was rare in his family until he, Tobias, and Taylor had formed the loser team championship.

Up until them, it seemed a Hamilton didn't marry unless the other person was the right one. They were hesitant to commit, but once they did, everyone in the family assumed it was permanent.

His ex didn't get the memo.

Leah's dark brown eyes bore into him. "I didn't know you were married before."

"Yeah."

Once again he read surprise and then the lowered eyebrows as she tried to picture him married with a white picket fence, a dog, and other shit.

"It wasn't my best idea."

"How long have you been divorced?" Damn, he shouldn't have opened that can of worms. Now her curiosity was peaked.

"A couple years, maybe five."

She sipped from her soda and then turned her plate sideways. "Have some of my fries."

Strange, no more questions. Instead she continued eating her hamburger while he drank from the newly refilled glass. In companionable silence, both in their thoughts, they finished the meal and he wondered if they'd go back to bickering over the property line once they got back to their ranches.

On impulse he tapped her hand. "Want to drive out to the mines? I planned to go out there to hike."

Surprise and then consideration. The woman was an open book. But she managed to surprise him with a nod. "Sure, I haven't been out there since high school." She blushed at pretty much admitting to having gone out there to make out.

In Laurel Creek, there were plenty of places to park out by the mines and back when he was a teen, every high schooler knew the lay of the land by the old mines.

Luke wondered if the new generations went there as well.

After paying the tab, they walked out in silence. He opened the passenger door to his truck so she could get in. Thankfully, she was wearing jeans and sneakers. As she stepped up into his truck, her pert ass took his attention. That part of her, he'd not studied before.

"Luke?" Leah had sat down and looked to him perplexed. "Something wrong?"

"Nah, just thinking we better grab some water before heading out."

WITH THE WINDOWS rolled down and the radio off, the sound of air and flapping of the wind through the interior of his truck filled the space.

Strange that he didn't feel awkward at remaining silent for long stretches of time when around Leah.

In his opinion, there was never a need to fill spaces with empty dribble. He slid a glance toward her noticing she scanned the surrounding landscape with a slight curve to her lips.

"Makes you wonder how any other state could top Montana when it comes to beauty," she said, not seeming to need a reply. "No matter where I travel, this place always takes my breath away."

Luke followed her line of sight to sloping hills where a few cows lingered. She was right. Many a night he'd fallen asleep while in the Middle East and dreamt of home.

They arrived at the gold mines. No other cars were about, so he ensured to pull over to a spot that over-looked the valley below. From there, they could catch sight of most of downtown Laurel Creek and the surrounding mountains. He'd forgotten how picturesque the view of his hometown was from there.

Funny how things looked different when one re-turned home. Things that were previously taken for granted, now stood out. Although jaded with people, he was not as much with Montana and what being home did for him.

"I'd forgotten about the view." Leah climbed out and rounded the truck to look out to the horizon.

Once he put four water bottles in a small backpack, he slung it over his shoulder. "Ready?"

"We're not going too far are we?"

"Nope, I gotta be back by five. Lawyer is coming over."

He knew the statement would bring out a reaction, so he purposely walked faster toward the mines. "Come on."

Leah caught up with him. He could feel her looking at him, but she didn't say anything. After a while, she started looking around, taking in the surroundings.

They walked for a mile or so before he stopped and crouched to study some animal prints. No need to put Leah in danger if there was a predator nearby.

Looked to be a coyote or wolf. Doubtful they'd at-tack.

"Is it about the land? The meeting today?"

He straightened and considered what Tobias would say about telling her about the visit. "Suppose so. Tobias arranged it. Takes a lot to make my brother mad. You seem to have an good inkling about what buttons to push with people."

You're such an asshole. Although she didn't say it out loud, her expression screamed it.

"It's an acquired talent," she replied wryly. "Don't waste your money, I'm dropping the issue. Probably go back to Billings."

"Giving up huh? You don't seem the type."

"What the hell do you think I should do? I don't have a job. This whole ranch thing was just a rouse to get rid of me. I don't need you to counsel me Luke. I need to relax, to figure things out."

Her eyes shined with tears and didn't that just make him feel like a total ass. She was right, he was the least qualified to say anything. His own shit was a long way from being together.

When she sniffed, he closed the distance between them to pull her close. No sooner did he wrap his arms around her did Leah slump against him. The woman was about as war-torn as anyone he'd seen in a long time. Of course her father had to have seen it too.

She had the look of someone becoming lost in work or whatever just to keep the monsters at bay.

Of course, this wasn't the time to tell her that no matter what one did, the bastards would remain.

Nothing, or no one, could kill his flashbacks nor the memories that popped up uninvited at the most random times.

She looked up at him. Her eyes moving to his lips and at the just so subtle invitation he lowered and took her up on it.

The kiss, which was all it was supposed to be, turned hungry, raw even. She raked her fingers up pushing his ball cap off.

Needing to feel more of her, he cupped her round ass with both hands and pulled her up against him. She wasn't a short woman, which suited the situation just fine.

He was hard as fuck within seconds of her pouty lips against his. Damn if the thought of how much he wanted them around his cock didn't make him even harder.

She slid her hands under his t-shirt and ran the soft palms across his back. The action stirred a need so deep, he moaned out loud.

They wouldn't progress to a point of lovemaking, not out there standing between rocks and for that he was thankful. The last thing he needed was the complication of any kind of expectance from her.

His mind whirled at the possibilities. He realized what had happened and took her by the upper arms to push her away. "Shit."

Both breathed heavily. His erection pulsed in his pants and she leaned forward and raked her fingers through her hair while blowing out a breath.

Luke walked a few feet and turned away. What the hell was he thinking bringing her here? From the first time seeing her when he'd gone to talk to her about the land issue, his curiosity had been peaked.

And now…now that he'd tasted, damn if he wasn't going to pursue her. Leah Morgan would be under him soon.

RAKING HER HAIR to the side, Leah attempted nonchalance while Luke kept his back to her. What was he thinking? Of course it had been on impulse. He was probably considering how to tell her he didn't find her remotely attractive, but had been driven to kiss her out of sympathy for her being so emotional.

Stupid drivel men usually said after an awkward happening never made any one but them feel better. She finally got her breathing under control enough to trust her voice. "That was stupid. Let's ignore it ever happened." Her chuckle came out dry. "Should we head back?"

When he turned, a storm brewed in his hazel eyes. "It wasn't stupid. We both wanted it, want each other. I'm fine with that."

Leah swallowed at his statement. Unable to stop from it, she took him in. The man was magnificent. A beautiful body, thick corded neck, wide shoulders and handsome beyond reason. Yes, she wanted him. Anyone with a brain wanted a man who looked like Luke Hamilton.

But it was more than that. He called to her, called to a part of her she'd sworn to keep locked up forever.

CHAPTER TEN

LUKE DIDN'T GIVE Toby Leah's message. It would be stupid not to hear what the lawyer had to say. Women were fickle, and after what had transpired between them, she could change her mind again. Especially since she didn't want to admit to wanting him. The hunger in her gaze was unmistakable. It wasn't the first time she'd imagined him naked. When he'd been on the couch the day she'd come over to look after his wounds, he'd seen it then. She imagined him lying on the couch totally bare, exposed to her.

Fair enough. He knew his body attracted women and most were curious as to what he looked like without clothes on. Whenever possible, he'd obliged them.

"He's here." Toby went to the door and opened it. Some things never changed. At spotting someone nearing, they always opened the door and a person stood outside waiting for the visitor to arrive.

"Hey Ernest," Toby called out in greeting.

The lawyer, Eric's brother, arrived with his dog in

tow. The tan Labrador ran in circles, tail wagging, ensuring everyone gave him the proper attention.

Their cousin stopped in his tracks at spotting Luke, and his expression shuttered. "I didn't know you were here."

"I can leave the room if it makes you feel better," Luke snapped. There was no love lost between them. They'd never gotten along and much less after the he'd slept with Ernest's girlfriend.

It had been wrong, although at the time, drunk and home on leave, he'd not thought it so bad. Over twenty years later, the guy still hated Luke.

Ernest ignored him, went to the table and opened a folder. "There isn't much of a case here. I called Mr. Morgan and said payment was unnecessary. He also said that if you insisted to donate the money to a veteran's organization. Once the paperwork is done up, he'll sign it."

"What about the shrew?" Toby asked, looking down at the papers.

"Don't," Luke said before he could stop. "I mean let's not go back to high school."

"Yeah, let's not." Ernest gave Luke a pointed look.

"No worries there. I am not attracted to Henry," Luke replied with a sneer. "He's safe around me."

Ernest had been in a relationship with a nice guy named Henry for almost ten years. Luke liked Henry way more than he did Ernest.

"I wouldn't put it past you."

"What the fuck man?" Luke got all up close and personal to his cousin. "Let it go already. Damn."

"Why because you don't like to be reminded what a fucking ass you are?"

"I don't need a reminder. And I don't need your stupid attitude every time I see you."

Ernest did not back away, but pushed against him, chest to chest. "Fuck you Luke."

Taylor who'd just walked in from working out, judging by his sweaty appearance, rushed to them. "All right everyone back to their corners." He turned to Ernest. "What the fuck are you doing? Don't provoke him."

"Whatever. I'm out of here." Ernest turned to Tobias. "Stop by with the signed papers. Leave your asshole brother behind."

Luke rushed his cousin, his fist slamming into the wise ass's mouth. Ernest recovered quickly and swung, landing a gut punch. Both exchanged a couple more before Toby and Taylor dragged them apart. Luke shook his right leg to dislodge the dog that'd attached himself gums deep into his calf.

"Get the damn dog off before I kick it." He let out a breath when Taylor pulled the dog back.

"Dumb to fight a guy when his dog's around," Taylor mumbled, dragging the growling dog to the doorway, while Ernest gave him one last glare.

"You heard Taylor, don't provoke me mother fucker." Luke flipped him off with both hands. Thankfully Tobias shoved Ernest back and slammed the door before turning to him.

"Very mature there brother."

Growling to release pressure, Luke swung away and headed to the kitchen. He went to the refrigerator and grabbed two beers and headed to the back porch. Thank goodness for jeans, or else the damn dog would have gotten a chunk out of his leg. There would however be a hummer of a bruise there now.

Within a minute or so, both beers were downed. He considered a third but decided against it, not wanting to go back inside and hear shit from his brother or cousin.

The back door opened and Tobias held out his phone. "Mom wants to talk to you."

There was challenge in his gaze and Luke returned it with a droll one. "You called her?"

"Yep."

"Ass…," he stopped hoping his mother didn't over-hear.

His mother talked to him for half an hour, encouraging him to get counseling and saying how he'd end up in jail if the anger issues continued. Same song, different melody. Coming from anyone else, he would have hung up, but Luke couldn't stand the thought of making his mother upset, so he promised to look into it.

The sun was setting as he got up and stretched. His entire body felt alive; the familiar sensations, the upcoming lack of control bubbled just beneath the surface.

Damn if he didn't just want to get in his truck and

drive until it fell off some edge. Thelma and Louise had something there.

"Police are here," Taylor called out from inside. "Tobias," he hollered out. "Did you get into it with Tori again?"

Luke didn't give enough of a shit to get up and see what a cop was there about. If anything, it was his cousin Eric coming to shoot the shit and not official business. Eric was Ernest's older brother, who like their father, continued the tradition of serving as law enforcement.

Personally Luke didn't get it. Glorified day care is what being a cop was all about.

"Hey." Eric's voice was without inflection, more on a flat note. "Need to talk to you."

What the fuck now? He racked his brain thinking of what the guy could possibly be wanting. Maybe there was some sort of arrest warrant out on him in Texas he didn't know about. Hell maybe the crackhead he'd beat the shit out of had died.

Luke considered what life in prison would be like and let out a breath. Wasn't too sure he could survive without open land.

His cousin lowered his large frame into a chair and propped his elbows on his knees. "What the fuck are you thinking attacking a lawyer?"

"Punk ass came to you?"

Eric's lips twitched. "My brother looks like shit and has cases to work. It doesn't look good for a lawyer to represent an abused wife with a busted lip and swollen eye."

"So, what do you want me to do? Go powder his nose?"

His cousin let out a breath and looked into the distance. "I need to retire. Spend more time with my horses."

Since it seemed he talked more to himself, Luke didn't say anything. Instead he followed Eric's line of sight. In the distance, the cows gathered under a small tree, several had lowered to the ground, no longer needing to graze.

ERIC HAD SEEMED similarly as dejected and ready to give up as him. Although lately he'd not felt the urge or drive to do much, once upon a time he'd had a brilliant career. He'd moved up quickly through the ranks in the Army. But life had a way of fucking up any plans, especially a future that included another person.

"I talked him out of pressing charges. But you need to apologize."

His attention came back to the situation. "It's best I don't go near him right now. The last thing I'm going to do is apologize to the asshole."

"He didn't ask that you do, and I'm not talking about today. I'm talking about the past. What you did was fucked up."

"And he needs to get the fuck over it." Luke stood. "Look Eric, you're a straight up guy. But your brother is a weasel. He only cares about himself and that pretend lifestyle he tries to build. The fucker should move to Los Angeles, he's better suited for one of those reality shows than life here in Montana."

"I'm not here to get into all that…"

"You just brought it up," Luke interrupted.

Eric let out a breath and stood up, his radio crackling with some shit that only a cop could understand. "I gotta go. Just think about it."

Thinking was one thing he wanted to avoid at the moment. Rounding the house, he stalked to his truck.

There was a cliff not too far away and he was about to drive right over it.

CHAPTER ELEVEN

THE ROOM WAS too empty, not of furnishings or décor. No, that wasn't what made it empty, it was the lack of sound. In the past, there had always been the sounds of conversation, or soft classical music her mother preferred in the background. The barking of dogs and footsteps of people moving about the house had filled every corner.

Now as Leah stared out through the kitchen window, silence pressed down on her like a waterlogged blanket.

One of her suitcases was on the floor in the middle of the room. Stuff strewn all around it as she'd hunted earlier for her portable speaker, needing to fill the house with sound. She'd found it, but the battery was dead, needed charging. Of course.

What was she going to do for six months? Her father wouldn't allow her to return for what seemed like an eternity. Of course, he couldn't stop her from working on her own, but what good would that do?

Had she turned into the person no one wanted to

work with? How long had people talked behind her back? The most important question was, why hadn't she known? Why hadn't she noticed the changes?

The familiar blue truck headed toward the house, dust in its wake from speeding over the uneven terrain.

Leah wondered what he wanted now, to argue again? She didn't have the energy to care enough to quarrel right now. What she wanted was noise, conversation, anything.

The truck disappeared around to the front and she didn't move. If Luke Hamilton wanted to find her, he'd have to come to her. She wasn't about to make it easy for the asshole.

Even though it was expected, when knocks sounded, she jumped. "Kiss my ass Luke Hamilton," she called out. "Go away."

The door opened. Damn it why hadn't she locked it?

His boots sounded on the hardwood floor, the sound almost music to her ears. Finally sounds other than her hollow voice. Nonetheless, she couldn't stop from scowling.

When she whirled around to throw him out, she collided with his broad chest.

Startled, she looked up to him. "What are you doing?"

"I want you."

When his mouth crashed with hers, Leah knew where things would lead. His low growl filled every corner of the space and she grasped his shirt, fisting the fabric to ensure he didn't move away.

THE MAN COULD kiss. Hunger and desperation melting every resolve, sending waves of heat through every limb until Leah could only cling to him. Her arms around his neck, she raked her fingers through his short hair and parted her lips to allow his tongue entrance.

Not just the feel of the hard, muscular body against hers, but also his roving hands sent tremors of need. As much as she wanted all clothing discarded, the anticipation of what was to come excited Leah. They would take their time, she'd ensure of it. The man had come to her, so she'd take full advantage.

She pushed him back and ran her palms down the wide expanse of his chest. He was built, muscular from hours spent working out. A good way to keep the demons at bay she guessed.

His chest lifted and fell with each breath, but he didn't move away, allowing her to do what she wanted. Doing her best to avoid the direct gaze, she instead concentrated on his body. With deliberate slowness, she slid her hands under his t-shirt, the heated skin against her palms more sensual than anything she remembered.

What was it about him? He'd called to her whether in a good way or bad way, she wasn't sure. Both were, just as strong. Since teens, she'd always known when he was near, sensed him.

When she reached his nipples, she circled them with

the tips of her fingers. The small buds peaked and he let out a low grunt.

Once again his mouth searched out hers, and she continued to play with his nipples enjoying the reaction of the hardening buds. It didn't last long, he yanked her against him and lifted her up. Wrapping her legs around his waist, she held on to him as his hips jutted forward pushing his hardness in between them.

Their mouths continued exploring, suckling and nipping, until want and desire raged so hot Leah didn't think she could withstand it.

Without hesitation, he carried her to the bedroom. Obviously, he'd caught sight of where it was the day he'd been injured as he now walked directly to the only room with a made up bed.

Luke lowered her to stand and stepped away. "Take your clothes off."

This was not lovemaking they were going to embark on. No reason for her to get any illusions. This was about sex, about getting off. That suited her just fine. And why the hell not, especially with someone who looked like him.

She kicked her shoes off, never taking her eyes off him, not wanting to miss the sight of him undressing. Leah removed her blouse and then her bra. Next, she bent to pull her jeans down her legs.

The direct gaze of his following her every move was almost as hot as his kisses. When he pushed his jeans and underwear down at the same time, her eyes widened.

Damn if he wasn't perfect.

His thick erection jutted from his body, demanding attention. She stared at his sex and her lips curved in anticipation.

Funny how other than the sentence he'd uttered, they'd not said anything else. Why bother? She preferred no promises, no stupid declarations of how pretty she was, or any other nonsense men felt the need to spew when anticipating a fuck.

Luke didn't try to make her feel better about what was happening. Both were perfectly aware of what it was.

When he moved closer, she stood next to the edge of the bed. For now she'd let him lead. Whatever he wanted to do was fine. Later it would be her turn.

He took her by the hips and guided her down onto the bed and onto her back. With her legs hanging off the side, he pushed them apart. When his mouth covered her sex, she bucked up in surprise.

Luke's tongue slid between her folds, sending instant awareness when he suckled and nipped ever so lightly at her clit.

"Shit!" Leah hissed out the word and grabbed the bedding with her hands in an attempt to stay grounded. He was relentless, his mouth moving over her sex going from sucking to flicking his tongue until she began to tremble.

His gaze lifted to her but before she could watch what he did, he pushed two fingers into her and she dissolved into quakes of release.

A cry sounded as she floated for a few seconds only to slam back down when he bit down on her inner thigh effectively starting another wave of sensations.

Luke trailed his tongue down the inside of her upper leg while he continued to slide his fingers in and out of her. She lifted her hips to meet his thrusts as cool air hit her exposed sex.

She almost cried when his mouth once again took her in and immediately she was lost to the abyss as a second climax hit.

Sliding his arms under her legs, he moved her to the center of the bed and rolled her to her stomach. Leah wanted to touch him, but he pushed her shoulders down with one hand and lifted her ass by sliding his right arm under her hips.

"I've got a condom," he informed her. His words were followed by the sound of foil being torn. She wiggled unsure of what to expect. He was so big and although she'd been with someone almost as large, it had been uncomfortable at times.

The tip of his cock nudged at her entrance and she pushed back wanting him inside. Even after two climaxes, the need returned. She needed to be lost in the only place no thought was needed.

Instead of entering her, he slid the tip up and down, from her sex to up between her butt cheeks. He then slid himself between her folds finding the perfect spot, sending tingles into her core.

"Ah. I want you," Leah sputtered. "Come on."

He remained silent and pressed wet kisses to her ass while his hands pulled her apart.

He was making sure she could take him.

Once again his fingers moved into her and she almost wept with relief. Although not enough, some of the building pressure left. She felt his hot breath on her lower back as he licked down her center, sending her right back to "fuck me now" town.

"Luke….please."

His grunt was followed by the tip once again teasing her entrance and he nudged just enough to let her know he tested.

Finally he plunged into her, with measured slowness, enough to allow her body to adjust, but also constantly forward until fully seated.

She let out a long breath and tried to relax, but the tension didn't allow it. She was stretched wide.

Luke pulled back just enough and pushed back in, each motion shoving her face into the bedding as he wasn't gentle. The man was about to take her fully, there was no mistaking it.

Holding her hips with both hands to keep her as steady as possible, he drove into her, pulling back almost entirely out before thrusting back in. She clawed at the bedding, the new sensations sending her over the edge. She'd never felt so completely filled by a man.

She wanted more, more of him, more of the sensations that coursed through her to continue without stopping. She mewled into the bedding unable to moan out loud.

Relentless, he didn't stop, but began moving faster. His thighs slapping against her ass, the sound as erotic as his low grunts.

When he pulled out, she looked over her shoulder at him. No, not now. Almost desperate, she rolled over and reached for him.

She rolled to her back and Luke climbed on top of her, his mouth taking hers as he pulled her arms over her head. She lifted up, wanting him inside again. He wasn't someone to be ruled in bed. Obviously the man would do what he pleased and how he pleased.

Almost crying with need, she twisted, attempting to pull her hands loose so she could take him. But instead, he pressed kisses down the side of her neck. For a moment he sucked at the apex of her neck and shoulder until Leah's eyes fluttered shut.

Every nerve so tight and aware, she could feel every inch where their bodies touched.

Luke took her left nipple into his mouth, sucking it hard. "Ah!" Leah once against tried to pull her hands free. The game of being held was so erotic she began shaking, unable to believe she was about to come from it.

When he moved to her right breast and nipped the tip with his teeth, she cried out, her body quaking in release.

The sound of his low chuckle the only indication he knew she'd come, but other than that, he was intent on exploring her fully.

Luke released her hands and rose over her straightening his arms. He looked down at her. "Look at me."

She complied and gasped. His bottom lip was split, fresh blood disappearing when he licked it away. There was bruising on the side of his left eye. He'd been in a fight recently.

However it was the darkened pools that took her attention. His eyes narrowed but he remained silent, studying her as if committing every aspect of her face to memory. He moved lower and then he lifted her legs up over his shoulders. "Tell me if it gets uncomfortable."

She watched with interest as he guided himself to her center, his gaze moving from her sex to her face. With deliberate slowness, he pushed in to her, once again the thickness filling her completely.

His mouth fell open as he moved out and back in. When she moaned, his eyes snapped to her face. "You okay?"

"Mmm hmm," she replied. "I'm good. More than good."

There was a slight lift to the corner of his lips as he proceeded to thrust forward. Obviously he'd not been all the way in, not at all. Leah cried out.

The sex turned frantic. The pace of his thrusts became faster and faster, as he pounded into her fully before pulling out, only to drive forward again. Then he lowered her legs and continued.

Past the point of reason, Leah clawed at his back and repeated the same sounds over and over as she flew so high it horrified her. She lost the fight to remain grounded and came so hard she almost blacked out. While screaming in release, her legs stretched out. No longer able to control herself, she could only flail as Luke continued his own trek to coming.

Finally, he groaned and trembled, his large body quaking as he came and she wrapped her arms around his waist to ensure he didn't move out. Not yet.

The sounds of their gulps and loud breaths seemed to echo in the air.

Straining over her, his heavy body was at the same time too much and not enough.

When he rolled away, the sudden vacancy was stark and Leah fought not to move closer to him.

She lay on her back staring up at the ceiling. *Don't leave*. The words repeated in her mind. *Not yet*.

"Shit." Luke's word was flat. Not divulging whether a thought or just something to say.

He sat up and turned to swing his legs over the side of the bed. In silence he dressed and she didn't watch this time. Instead, she got up and grabbed a discarded robe pulling it on and tying the belt tight around her middle.

"See you around." He walked out of the bedroom.

She followed after him. "I doubt it."

When his gaze met hers, she thought to have seen something flicker, but probably just her imagination. He lifted his chin just a bit. "You leaving town?"

"Not yet."

He looked past her. "Thanks."

"Don't come back."

Instead of a reply, he gave a subtle nod and walked straight out the front door.

CHAPTER TWELVE

IT WAS SUPPOSED to have made him feel better. Luke had driven back home, went directly past the front room where Tobias watched television, and straight to the bedroom. He yanked off his clothes and made a beeline for the shower.

Hot water steamed up the room fast as he ran a bar of soap over himself removing any remnant of her scent.

He'd not made love…correction, fucked like that before. He'd prolonged it, not wanting it to end. Hell, he'd almost come just by eating her.

What the hell was all that about? She wasn't the first beautiful woman he'd slept with. However, it had been a long time since he had been with someone so right, a perfect match for him.

Every inch of her body had appealed to him in a way that was new. Even with the ex, who he'd fallen so hard for, it had never been like that. This experience had the potential to be addicting. Good thing she set him straight afterwards.

It had been a one-time thing.

Yeah…good. Whatever.

She'd called out his name.

"Ugh." Luke finished washing his junk, rinsed and cut the water off.

"YOU GOING TO work today?" Tobias was in the kitchen the next morning when Luke walked in from his bedroom. Already dressed and looking about to head out, his brother drank from a coffee cup and watched him over the brim. "You know the rules."

"I'll be out there. What's going on today?"

Nobody slouched at the Hamilton Ranch. There was always work to do and everyone knew the number one rule. You stay, you play.

"Taking twenty to the slaughterhouse and separating the herd to two areas." Tobias put the cup down and walked to the door. "See you in ten."

IT FELT NATURAL to be on horseback chasing after cows. In the distance Taylor used a four-wheeler to do his tasks.

The horse Luke rode wasn't his. He didn't own a horse. Since his died while he was gone, he'd had never taken the time to pick another one out. However the one he rode currently was the same one as the day before, and he liked the animal. It was high strung and ready to kick ass, a perfect match for his own personality.

In the distance, Tobias called out riding in circles around the other portion of the herd. It was evident by the ease in which he managed his mount, he'd been doing so regularly. Although Luke prided himself in horsemanship, he could not compete with his twin. The boy could ride.

A thought struck as Luke rode toward some stragglers. This was the type of thing a man could get lost in. Working hard all day, forgetting and letting go of the past. It didn't matter that the demons waited, he could keep them at bay.

He'd slept soundly the night before after coming back from Leah's place. The same would happen this night. All he had to do was work hard and keep himself busy.

Montana was the counseling he needed.

The ranch was his medication and cure.

FOR TWO NIGHTS he'd slept deeply, without dreams or the haunting memories that crept up without warning. Not enough to call victory, but Luke felt more rested than he had in years. The crisp morning air blew across his face as he drank coffee on the back porch, his eyes following the progress of two dogs that ran in circles. Tongues lolling to the side of their mouths, the pups enjoyed the game of chase, their antics entertaining.

"Wanna go into town tonight?" Taylor walked past him and to the dog's excitement began rough housing with them.

Could he even consider that normalcy was within reach? Taylor had his own monsters to slay, yet the guy kept an easygoing way about him. There were different ways to keep the past at bay Luke supposed.

"Where you going?"

Taylor turned to where he stood and lowered his brows. "Probably the pool hall. Either there or Ed's Barbeque."

"I'm game. Don't feel like cooking."

THE PARKING LOT at the barbeque was packed and immediately Luke reconsidered the outing. Just because he'd had a good couple of days didn't mean it was time to be around lots of people. He and Taylor always had a way of finding trouble. If they didn't find it, the bastard would come looking for them.

Seeming to have the same thought, Taylor looked to him and adjusted his ball cap. "Want to go somewhere else?"

"I'm good."

"Say the word and we're out." Damn if his cousin didn't make him feel better. Family could suck, but he could always count on Taylor and Tobias. Although Tobias was more the tough love kinda guy.

The smell of smoke and barbeque sauce was strong and his stomach rumbled in return. They found a corner table and it was comical as both considered who'd get to sit with his back to the wall. Taylor rolled his eyes and let Luke take the seat. "It would look stupid for us to sit side by side," he grumbled and pulled out a chair on the other side of the table.

A teenage girl came over, her bored expression not changing as she pulled a pad from a stained apron pocket. "Know what you want?"

"Two pig out plates and I'll take a beer," Taylor said then looked to Luke.

"Water's fine."

The teen looked to him from the side of her eyes. "I heard you beat up Ernest."

"We beat up each other," Luke replied. "Why is that news?"

She shrugged. "Cause he put my brother in jail. I can't stand him."

He could certainly understand why. But decided it was best to keep his opinion to himself. "Bet he deserved it," he said and the teen shook her head.

"Whatever."

Taylor looked over his shoulder. "I thought Ernest stayed away from that kind of case. I should get out more. Don't know who's doing what anymore."

"Do you really give a shit about it?"

"No, but my mother does. She asks me about it when I visit."

The subject of Taylor's parents was not discussed unless he brought it up. Taylor's father was dead, killed by his mother. And although most thought Taylor should hate her, he visited her in prison monthly. Whether to torture himself or her, wasn't clear. His comment surprised Luke, as Taylor said it almost as if he and his mother remained close.

"Any chance she'll get out soon?"

"Nope. Got life."

"I wonder sometimes if I'll end up in prison," Luke said, uttering the words before he thought better of it. When Taylor looked at him, it was clear the thought had occurred to his cousin as well.

They remained silent as the sullen teen returned with plates piled high with meat, beans and coleslaw. "Refills?

Luke raised an eyebrow. "I would say yes, but you never brought drinks."

"Oh shit." She raced off as they both dug into their food.

In between bites, Taylor spoke. "Toby kept expecting to hear you were arrested and getting locked up for murder or something because of your issues. Have to admit, we wouldn't have been surprised."

He didn't want to talk about it. Why the hell had he brought it up to begin with? "Yeah, I know."

"Can't keep a job. You lose your temper at the drop of a hat. Heard you beat the shit out of some guy in Tucson and that's why you got fired from the trucking job."

"Bastard had it coming."

Taylor met his gaze. "Is that so?"

The fight had been over some truck stop hooker. The guy had slapped the woman and he'd interceded. His interrupting the abuse was not wrong. What had been totally bad was that he couldn't stop hitting once he started. Turned into an abuser beating the shit out of another one.

"I'm trying. That's why I'm here."

"Aaaand, you beat the shit out of Ernest."

"He's an asshole."

"Gotta agree with you there. Doesn't excuse it."

And this was the part where his cousin would tell him to get help and how counseling would help. How he couldn't deal with it alone…blah blah blah bullshit.

"Ever consider MMA or something? You can beat the shit out of people and it's cool."

"No. I don't want to mess up my pretty face."

They chuckled and once again Luke was glad to have his cousin as a friend. "Wanna go to Shooters?"

Shooters was a pool hall and club combo on the edge of town.

"Sounds like a plan."

CHAPTER THIRTEEN

"NO." Leah's resolve was wavering. Allison had been there for two days and they'd yet to go anywhere.

Her friend had arrived with boxes of décor and props. They'd spent the past several hours doing photo shoots and decorating the house. The rooms were transformed, and although reluctant, Leah had to agree it felt more like a home now.

"My neck hurts from all those weird poses you put me in for your pictures."

Allison gave her a droll look. "I love taking pictures here. It's a blank canvas." Her friend pursed her lips. "Let's grab pizza and then we're going to listen to some live music." She stood up. "Go put on some tight jeans and a low cut blouse. We're going man hunting."

Immediately a picture of a very naked Luke sprung to mind. She'd yet to stop thinking of how good it had been. The man definitely knew how to make an impression. It had been the best sex ever and as much as it pained her, she craved him.

"I'm not hunting for men. Too much trouble."

"Ha!" Allison gave her a pointed look. "That's an understatement. We're not going to keep them. We'll trap them, fuck them, and release them back into the wild."

Leah shook her head and smiled. "Since you put it that way. I better bring some rope."

THE ATMOSPHERE IN Shooters brought back memories of dancing and enjoyment. It wasn't until last year of high school and after her first years of college when she visited, that she and her friends would come there. Remembering the horrible headaches, she vowed not to have more than a couple drinks.

It was easy to find an empty table. Because Laurel Creek was a tiny place, the younger crowed preferred to travel the hour to Billings to party.

"Holy shit," Allison said, looking around. "This place has not changed one bit."

With a line of pool tables along one wall, a bar against the other, the open space was indeed the same as Leah remembered. Along the right side there were booths, and tables were scattered in the center. A small stage and dance floor in the back right corner completed the look.

No matter what a person wanted, whether to stand out by sitting in the center or at the bar, or to blend by sliding into a darker booth, it could be accomplished there.

"We've got wings now." A guy arrived at their booth. "If you want some."

"A beer and a pile of spicy wings sound good." Allison grinned up at the guy who winked in return.

"I'll take a light beer and a hot dog all the way please," Leah said when he turned his attention to her. "Make that two dogs."

The guy swaggered away as they both watched.

"Cutie." Allison swung back to Leah. "Tell me about Luke again."

The woman had been relentless since she'd told her about Luke falling through the roof and how much he'd changed. Leah had left out sleeping with him. If she'd told Allison, her friend wouldn't stop until she got every detail and then she'd insist they were in love or some crazy thing like that. Allison was a diehard romantic.

They drank beers and chatted about this and that for a few minutes. Finally the server returned.

"Holy shit," Allison said in a reverent tone. "That's a lot of wings." The cute guy slid a long plate with a mound of chicken before her friend and a plate with hot dogs in front of Leah.

Leah immediately picked up her hotdog and took a healthy bite. After washing it down with the ice-cold beer, she had to agree this was a good idea. "I'd forgotten how good the food was here." She nabbed one of Allison's wings.

"The sights aren't so bad either," Allison replied, her eyes widening. "Hot damn."

Somehow Leah didn't have to look to know Luke was there. Of course, the one night she decided to get out, he would be out as well. From what she knew, he was pretty much a hermit.

Not a good thing he and she were there at the same time. Somehow, she doubted luck would be with her and they'd not have to talk. Then of course there was the matter of no one knowing they'd slept together.

"Hey guys!" Allison waved her hand and looked to Leah. "Taylor and his cousin, Lukey boy, just walked in."

"Great." She couldn't keep the annoyance from her voice. "Why'd you call them over?"

"Hi." Taylor, who neared first, grinned down at Allison and then looked to her. Of course the grin disappeared given they'd just gone through the whole property line thing. "What's up ladies?"

Luke remained silent, his hands shoved into his pockets. He looked from them toward the bar.

"Came out for a bite," Allison answered returning the smile. "Wanna join us?"

Kicking her friend would be obvious, so instead Leah looked to Luke. "How are the cuts and bruises?"

The corners of his lips twitched. "Not bad. My lips took longer than the rest to heal. Kinda strange."

Heat rushed to her face and she looked to Taylor who was saying something she couldn't hear past the thudding of her heart echoing in her ears. The two walked away and she looked to Allison. "Why would you invite them to join us?"

Allison laughed. "I knew they wouldn't, just wanted to see how they'd react."

"You're crazy."

She tracked the men who walked to the bar and talked to the guy behind it who handed them both a bottle of beer. Moments later beers in hand, they went to the pool tables.

Taylor had said Tobias was gone to his parents for the night. Interesting that Luke had not joined his brother, but what the hell did she know. Although they'd been intimate, she didn't know crap about Luke Hamilton.

"What was the deal with you two?" Allison watched her. "There was something there between you and Luke."

"Dislike? Annoyance? Or could it be the fact he antagonizes me constantly?"

"Nope," Allison replied, looking to where Luke and Taylor now played pool. "He's very interested in you. If I didn't know better, I'd guess you two had totally been naked together."

"You don't know better. And yeah, so not happening."

Thankfully Allison dropped the subject when a pair of women walked in. Although it was much too cool for it, one wore shorts and the other a short sundress. Both wore cowboy boots and from the tossing of hair came for more than just food and drinks. The duo made a beeline for the pool table where Luke and Taylor played.

After some interaction, mostly with Taylor, the guys continued to play with a rapt audience of two.

The loud oohs and laughter grated every one of Leah's nerves. "She has the most annoying laugh." Leah slid a look toward the pool tables. "I can hear her over the music."

Allison nodded. "The guys are about to get lucky. They don't even have to try hard. In the mean time, me and you may strike out."

"I don't want to get lucky," Leah said tapping the table for emphasis. "You however can, there's a good-looking guy over at the bar."

After a quick look over her shoulder, Allison shook her head. "Nah, I think he's drowning his sorrows and will be sloppy drunk by the time he leaves."

Four guys walked in. From their dusty boots and dirty clothes, they'd just left work. One of them looked to where the foursome at the pool tables talked and stopped walking midstride.

"Oh-oh," Allison whispered. "Something's up."

The guy was a large man, not as muscular as Taylor or Luke, but he made up for it in burliness. He stormed over to the pool table area with the other three forming some sort of guard behind him.

"What the fuck you doing here Donna?"

"Shit we should go." Leah started to slide out only to

be stopped by Allison grabbing her arm.

"Are you crazy. This is going to be fun. I can't wait to see who throws the first punch." Her friend clapped with glee earning a glare from an older pair of women who signaled for the waiter to bring their checks.

Meanwhile, Donna, the girl in the shorts, held up a middle finger and huffed. "None of your business. What I do is none of your concern Bobbie. We're done."

Bobbie wasn't having it. He clenched his hands into fists. "Get the fuck away from those assholes."

"Make me!" Donna screamed and laughed. She looked to her friend who didn't seem to find any humor in the situation.

The sundress girl tugged at Donna's arm. "Lets get out of here."

"Fuck no!" Donna said to no one in particular.

The husky guy spat on the floor and rolled his neck. "Come on Donna. We're going home."

Taylor stepped forward. "I don't think the lady wants to go with you. Leave her be."

"I don't have a beef with you Taylor, so you best just step aside. Donna, I'm telling you one more time…"

Donna rushed forward and slapped the guy so hard, the sound seemed to echo. The older ladies screamed and rushed out and Leah looked to Allison. "Great."

The husky guy backhanded Donna so hard, the woman flew back into Taylor who in turn stumbled backwards.

Until that point, Luke had remained in the background. With a growl, he rushed forward, his arms out from his body, eyes locked to the husky man. Something about his demeanor sent the guy's three buddies to take steps backward.

He slammed his fist into the guy's jaw so hard, the burly guy's head slanted down to his shoulder.

"No Luke!" Taylor yelled and tried to push his cousin aside while waving at the guys. "Get out of here now!"

Too late. The second punch made the husky guy bend forward with a loud wooshing sound from deep in his lungs. It was followed by a third and fourth hit, which were so fast, Leah could not keep up.

"Get him the fuck out of here now!" Taylor yelled and tried to grab Luke's arm. However Luke was beyond stopping, pounding bloody fists into the guy's face and then hitting any of the others who tried to intervene.

Finally Taylor took a running start and tackled Luke sending him several feet crashing into tables and chairs. A pair of guys who'd been playing at another table watched silently from against the wall.

"Holy shit," Allison said, her eyes wide. She and Leah were now standing on top of the booth seats, doing their best to blend into the wall behind them.

Leah could not tear her eyes away from the raging beast Luke had become. He swung at Taylor who was quick enough to get out of the way. Outside, sirens sounded and Leah hoped the police would get there before anyone else got hurt.

Luke stalked toward Taylor who now held his hands up ready to defend himself.

"Both of you, get the fuck out of here." The bartender held up a bat, not moving from behind the bar.

The young guy who'd been Leah and Allison's server stood next to the bar watching, seeming more entertained than afraid.

Face contorted with rage, Luke faced the doors just as two police officers entered with guns drawn.

"Get down on the floor you two," one of the police officers called out. "Now!"

His moves mechanical, Luke complied while Taylor looked to one of the officers. "Don't handcuff him. Call Eric."

Why all the instructions? Why did it seem as if Taylor feared what his cousin was capable of while at the same time protecting him?

"Hands behind your back," the officer replied.

"Please," Taylor said following instructions and keeping his gaze on Luke. "He has PTSD and can't control his rage. Do as I say, he could hurt you."

A third police officer rushed to Luke. Bad idea, just as a loud growl sounded Luke swung sending the guy realing back into his partner. Both men fell backwards cursing loudly.

Luke stood his chest heaving with each breath and shoulders hunched forward prepared for anything.

"Get on the floor now!" One of the officers yelled the ear splitting sound of a gun being fired followed the command.

This time, both Leah and Allison screamed.

CHAPTER FOURTEEN

*R*ED. *EVERYTHING WAS red and all he could hear was blood rushing. There was the tunnel, the short bridge. "Stop! Pull back! Pull back!"*

Luke's throat was raw from screaming and yet they kept moving forward, the oppressive heat surrounded and pressed down on him like a furnace. The scorching temperature not abating until he thought he'd pass out from it. "I said pull back!" The command came out a hoarse whisper, not the loud bark he normally used to order the troops with. What was wrong with him?

He grabbed at the man next to him only to come up empty. His hands flailing through emptiness. The next explosion was not like other times, deafening until his ears bled. This time it was like an echo, the sound vibrating through him sending him through the air until he landed so hard the wind was knocked out of him.

As hard as he struggled to get up, to go and help the others, he couldn't move. Every limb was locked in place arms stuck to his sides and he fought and fought until the saltiness of his tears and sweat covered his face.

Darkness fell, it always did.

"No!" He had to help them, had to save them.

"Luke. Honey wake up." His mother's soft voice penetrated through the thick fog that enveloped. Luke tried to talk, but his tongue was thick and heavy.

"Here." A straw was pushed past his cracked lips and he sucked greedily loving the feel of cold liquid that flowed down his throat. Still he could barely pry his eyes to more than slits.

He was in a hospital that much he could tell. The fluorescent lights overhead were so blinding, he squeezed he eyes shut.

"I'll lower the lights," his mother said and the room was immediately dimmed, only sunlight coming through the one large window.

He tried to sit up, but couldn't move.

"You're restrained. Don't try to move, you'll hurt yourself more."

More?

There wasn't any pain, as far as he could tell anyway. Somewhere in the recesses of his mind, he recalled a fight. He'd tried to intervene in a domestic dispute.

"Damn it." His raspy voice was countered by a need to clear his throat. "What happened? Did I…"

"You got into a fight. Lost control. They had to Taser you. As hard as the doctors tried, they couldn't bring you out of the rage, so they had to use sedatives after they brought you here."

"Where?"

"Luke?" His father leaned over him. "It's time for this to stop. You're staying here, and if I have my way, strapped down until you listen to reason."

"Really John? Do you have to do this now?" His mother tried to stop his dad, but they both knew it was useless. One thing about the Hamilton's, they were strong and stubborn as hell.

His dad frowned. "You hear me boy. That's it. I've had enough of trying to give you time. The only thing that's going to accomplish is you killing someone."

The door opened and Luke groaned. Who was it now? He felt like a damn zoo animal on display. The rare raving maniac species. Yet he didn't dare say anything. He wouldn't cuss in front of his mother and the words on the tip of his tongue were not for her ears.

"I see he's awake." A doctor neared and took the top off a syringe. "This will keep you calm for a bit. Until the physiologist gets here tomorrow, we'll keep you sedated Mr. Hamilton."

"No."

"You lost your choice in the matter I'm afraid." The doctor looked to his parents. "Police got a judgment. You're under arrest and considered dangerous unless sedated."

He pounded his head back on the pillow, immediately regretting it when the urge to throw up caused him to cough and gag.

"Leave the room for a bit," the doctor instructed and motioned a nurse forward. Pushing the bed's buttons, they lifted him to sitting. Just in time a trashcan was placed against his chest as he threw up.

The doctor stood by the door. "You may want to stay steady. You can have water, but that's it for the time being."

How the fuck was he supposed to drink? Luke was glad when the nurse helped him take water from a glass and rinse out his mouth. Afterwards he pushed his head back against the pillows and glared at the blank television.

The nurse adjusted his bed back a bit. "Its best you stay a bit upright until the nausea passes. You okay for now?" She had kind eyes.

Luke nodded. "Yeah I'm good. Thank you."

LATER THAT NIGHT, he watched a game as Tobias snored in the chair next to the bed. He'd tried to kick his brother out, but the guy insisted on staying. One good thing about it was he didn't have to get a nurse to help him pee. On the other hand, Tobias made fun of him the entire time.

What an ass.

"Toby," he said in a loud voice.

Tobias' head snapped up and unfocused eyes searched his face. "Yeah…what? You okay?"

"Untie me. I have to go to the bathroom."

His brother rolled his neck and looked to the door. "Nah. You'll make a break for it."

"I'm not fucking around man. I have to take a crap."

"Shit."

"Untie me. I won't go anywhere."

One thing both prided themselves on was never breaking a promise. So his brother loomed over him. "Promise, you'll come right back to bed. I don't want to have to kick your ass."

He rolled his eyes. "I don't need anymore trouble. Rather be here than at the jailhouse. I promise."

Once he went, Luke walked back and stared down at his hospital gown. Ass hanging out the back and black socks didn't exactly make good escape attire. "Where's my clothes?"

"Mom took them." Toby stood with his back to the door, arms crossed. "Get back in bed."

Feeling lightheaded, he did as his brother instructed and lifted the back to sitting. "Like I said, I'm not going anywhere. Who pressed charges? Where's Taylor?"

"They arrested you both, or Taylor anyway for public endangerment and drunk and disorderly. Taylor spent the night in jail. Mom and Dad refused to go get him."

"We weren't drunk. Taylor didn't do anything."

"Yeah he did. He tackled the cop that was going to handcuff you."

How much longer would other people pay for his problem? The issue was his own and Luke didn't have a problem with that, but when his family got hurt or involved, the game changed. And didn't that just make him feel like shit.

"I thought I heard a shot. Anyone get hurt?"

Tobias sat down, with his elbows resting on the bed next to Luke's leg. He looked him straight in the eye. "Not this time. Eric came in and shot at the ceiling to get everyone's attention. He might be in trouble too. Man you have to do something. I get it. I know why you intervened. The problem is you can't stop."

He couldn't. No matter how many times he repeated to himself the flashbacks were under control, once he saw red, all control was lost.

"They died. I didn't. Sometimes I think they are the lucky bastards. I'm left with shit I can't control. Every day I have to walk the tightrope keeping my balance and praying nothing sets me off. What kind of life is that? Why do I even keep hanging on?"

"You didn't die. Who knows why." Tobias straightened. "I know where you're coming from. There are times I'm back in Iraq, times when the shakes get me so hard my teeth rattle. Thank God no one died on my watch, so I have no idea about that. But I will tell you this brother... you have to do something. And I don't mean put a gun to that block head of yours."

"Your head is just as huge."

Tobias let out a huff and looked up to the ceiling. "Being your twin sucks. I mean it." He looked to the door. "Our cuz is actually going to the judge tomorrow to see about dropping charges for you. He wants to say you're getting counseling."

Luke bit back the "hell naw," and instead clenched his jaw. How many times would he sit in a damn circle and listen to others whine about how shitty their lives were? How the hell was that going to help? He could go back to taking the drugs. Walk around in a stupor. Who gave a shit anyway?

"Yeah fine. But this time, I am not going to one of those support groups. I'm going to find a doctor myself. And you're going too."

Toby's mouth fell open. "Since when is this about me?"

"Stop lying Tobias. You know damn well, you didn't go to Iraq, patrolled the fucking streets of Fallujah, and never lost one person. Someone fuckin' died and you well know it. Stop painting it like you went camping or some shit."

His twin's jaw clenched and his nostrils flared. "You don't know shit. I'm not the one losing it every other day. I don't go around beating the shit out of every damn body."

"The nurses asked me to come and see what was going on." A large man stood at the door. Scrubs didn't hide the guy's muscular body. Obviously he was the night shift nurse/bodyguard. "Keep it down." The male's eyes went to Luke's wrists.

"Why aren't you restrained? The nurses won't come in here if you're not tied up." He neared the bed slowly and pulled Luke's arm to the side. "I'll keep them loose."

Luke lowered his gaze and focused on the foot of the bed. He could feel Toby watching. Even angry, his brother would ensure he kept his cool.

"I let him get up to go to the bathroom. He'll be fine without restraints for now." Toby tried to convince the nurse, but within moments, he was once again restrained.

The guy looked Luke over, his eyes flat. "Once the psychologists gives the order, we can go from there. For now, you have to remain restrained." He looked to Tobias. "Please don't do it again or we'll have to not allow visitors."

After the nurse left, Luke tugged at the restraints, more out of habit than anything else as he was sure they were pretty secure.

"Ever been tied up in bed?" He looked to his twin. "I haven't."

Tobias gave him a droll look. "If I have, you're the last person I'd admit it to."

"So the answer is yes. Kinky bastard."

"You're an idiot." Tobias settled down into the chair and lifted his feet up to Luke's bed. "Go to sleep.

"WE WILL START with cognitive behavioral therapy combined with antidepressants," the psychiatrist said, his gaze moving from Luke to his brother. "Since you prefer not to talk in a group setting, then we will avoid it for now. I am also going to ask that you stay out of places where groups gather and for the time being stick to familiar places that won't trigger any strong emotions. Home, work, and maybe a once a week trip to town, but only to a small business or such. As soon as you feel a trigger, you leave."

He liked the guy. Unlike the quacks back in Texas, this guy was older and from the direct way he spoke, wouldn't take any shit from him. Something about the doctor put Luke at ease.

Although he felt like a loser for not being able to control himself, the doctor didn't back down nor did he try to talk Luke out of the belief a lot of what happened was his fault.

They'd not talked other than general stuff, so his perceptions could still change. Sometimes these people had a way of coming across one way until you started talking more and then the demands would come.

"I'm not sure about taking any kind of drugs. I don't want to walk around in a fog. I'm a rancher, can't risk my horse or my brother and cousin."

The man nodded. "Totally get that. I'm prescribing Prozac. After a few days of feeling like everything is groovy, you'll adjust and it shouldn't affect your reactions nor will you feel out of it."

"I might want some of that," Toby cut in. The doctor looked at his brother. "You want to talk to me? We can set up a time."

Toby's grin disappeared, replaced with a blank look

that reminded Luke of when his brother got grounded. "Nah, this is about my brother."

There was more blah, blah, blah and Luke wanted to tell the doctor to get out of his face. The guy seemed to know his shit and he didn't doubt talking to him would help, but nothing would cure him. The monsters in his closet were there to stay.

"Luke," the psychiatrist, Doctor Sullivan, pinned him with a direct look. "If you're thinking I can't help you get rid of the crap, you're right. But what I can do is show you how to deal with it so you can manage your reactions to situations better."

Luke nodded, not at all comfortable with how easy the guy could read his mind.

"Yeah, we'll see doc."

CHAPTER FIFTEEN

"I T'S BEEN TWO weeks. You have to admit, it was an unforgettable night out," Allison laughed over the speaker on Leah's cell phone. "What happened to the guys?

The last thing Leah wanted to do at the moment was rehash the night at Shooters. But Allison seemed to think it had been the adventure of a lifetime.

Other than the gunshot scaring the crap out of her, she'd been transfixed by the occurrence. She'd tracked every one of Luke's movements, amazed and horrified at how out of control he'd become. The guy needed help. At the same time, she'd also seen the gentler more caring side of him. There was the out of control Luke and the guy who'd offered to climb up on the roof to check out a noise that scared her.

"Even if it was entertaining, someone could have been seriously hurt. And I'm not so sure I trust Luke Hamilton anywhere near me. The guy has serious anger management issues." Leah let out a breath. "I think I'm coming back to Billings. I'm throwing in the towel on this place."

She looked around the large living room. The house was beautiful, so full of memories it made her heart ache for simpler times. Although interested buyers and a couple of realtors had stopped by, she'd been unable to list the house and land for sale. It felt wrong, like a betrayal to her ancestry.

"Why don't we plan a spa weekend? Maybe if you get away for a couple days, you can go back and get a new perspective." Allison always insisted getaways cleared the mind and were the cure for everything.

Leah looked out the picture window to the road leading to the house. No one had been there in three days. She'd gone to town several times just to have interaction with other people. "It's so damn quiet here. I need a dog or two. Maybe I should get a cat. Wonder if I can borrow some kids to run around."

"Holy shit. You thinking about having a kid now? Who's going to be the daddy?"

She couldn't help but laugh. "No kids, I'm way past that stage."

"Nah. Janet Jackson had a baby. Isn't she like fifty?"

The conversation as always went down rabbit trails and Leah was glad to have steered Allison away from the night Luke and Taylor had been arrested.

They ended the call with her promising to consider the spa weekend just as a truck appeared in the distance. A blue truck.

She held her breath and rushed to the window. It was unfortunate that both Toby and Luke had the same color truck, so she couldn't tell who came. Toby's was newer and a bit lighter, but that wouldn't help much since most of the time both were dusty.

When Tobias climbed out she let out a breath and her stomach settled. Had she been hoping it was Luke?

She walked out to the porch just as Tobias approached. Greeting her with a crooked grin, so unlike his brother, he approached but didn't climb the steps to the porch.

"Hey Leah."

She greeted him wondering why he was there, but not wanting to ask. "Hey."

"Luke asked me to come by and check on you. He's been after me for days, but I've been busy with work and all." He kicked at a rock. "Should have come sooner to make sure you didn't get too spooked after what happened."

Words caught in her throat. Of all the things, this was unexpected. "I'm fine. It was a bit scary, but not much more than when you guys got in fights at Shooters back in the day."

He met her gaze with both brows lifted. "This was nothing like that. I know my brother lost control. The war messed him up."

Two rockers Allison had insisted they buy for curb appeal came to good use as she motioned to them. They settled into them and Tobias stretched his legs out. She couldn't help but wonder why, although he was physically identical to Luke, she didn't feel the same attraction to Tobias. Yes, they had the same face, but Tobias didn't have the same attitude. His expressions were softer and there was an easy-going air about him that immediately differentiated him from his twin.

"What happened to him? Why is he like that? He's a…"

"He's an asshole." Tobias chuckled. "Lots of shit happens over there. Stuff that we can't just push away and not think about it." He got a faraway look and Leah could tell he was considering what exactly to share. Tobias had served as well, but he'd been discharged early after their father had a heart attack and he'd refused to reenlist. That's when he took over the ranch.

Toby's next statement made Leah gasp. "Luke is pissed off because he was the only survivor of a bomb attack. He feels guilty and doesn't know how to deal with it."

"Why would he feel guilty? It's not his fault…"

"He was in charge and he made the decision to go that specific route on that day." Tobias blew out a breath. "I feel bad for my brother. War's a bitch."

She couldn't imagine the burden he carried. "What's happening now? How's Taylor?"

"The judge took it easy on Taylor after his lawyer explained the reason he pushed the officer way. So he's good. Luke's getting counseling. So far, so good."

"I appreciate you coming here to check on me. I'm

good. Still trying to decide what to do with the place." Leah followed Tobias' line of sight as he looked across the flat front yard toward the road.

"Yeah, I bet it's hard to sell, once you acknowledge that it's part of you." He shrugged. "So you're not as much of an asshole as I thought you were."

"Gee thanks," she grumbled. "Nice of you to notice." Admittedly she'd been over the top and demanding regarding the land issue. Anger over her career situation had brought out the worst in her.

"If you decide to sell, let us know. We might be interested. I think Luke has decided to stay here."

Selling to the Hamiltons had occurred to her. They could expand and have a second house. But the thought of Luke living there caught her off guard and she couldn't stop the picture of remaining there too.

"I will."

Toby stood and stretched. "I better get back. Luke's cooking, so it's gonna be good."

"He told me he cooks a lot."

"He's good…why don't you join us?" Toby gave her a wide grin. "Not like you have plans or anything right?" He motioned to the truck. "Come on I'll drive ya."

There was no polite way to say no and she wanted to see Luke. The glutton for punishment in her wanted to see a man who was not just dangerous in general, but exactly the opposite of any man she ever wanted to be associated with.

"Okay."

IT WAS A short drive to the Hamiltons, not enough time to get her thoughts in order nor did she have time to plan what to say or how to act. Although she'd made it clear to Luke their hook up was a one-time thing, it could be awkward to be in the same room with him surrounded by people that knew them both.

Moments later, Tobias was rounding the truck to let her out. Two labs bounded to greet them and she stopped to pat their heads. "Come on boys," Tobias called to the dogs that followed them into the house.

The aroma filling the space was like that of a high priced restaurant. Leah took in a deep breath. "It smells amazing."

"I know, right?" Tobias grinned. "Come on, how about a glass of wine or something."

She followed his broad back, while taking a deep breath and hoped for a look of nonchalance.

Luke was chopping vegetables when they walked into the large kitchen. His eyes widened at seeing her before moving to Tobias. There as some sort of communication between the twins. Leah was pretty sure, her being there did not make Luke happy.

"How are you?" She made sure to look him straight in the eyes. "Smells incredible. So glad Tobias invited me over, it would have been another grilled cheese sandwich and soup day for me."

"You could learn to cook." Luke barely spared her a glance.

"Here you go." Tobias placed a glass of red wine in

front of her. "Hope you like Cab, it's all we have. Mom's favorite."

"Cab's great, thanks."

Taylor walked in and stopped dead in his tracks. He looked to her, then to his cousins. "Oh hey. I didn't know we had company." Shirtless in low hung sweats, he seemed to have just walked out of the shower. Leah didn't mind the view one bit. He was a hunk.

"Man, throw on a shirt," Luke growled at his cousin and Leah wanted to laugh at Taylor's expression when he turned back to her.

"Uh...yeah. You joining us for dinner?"

Leah nodded. "Yes, Tobias invited me."

"Awesome. Luke's a great cook."

"So I hear." She looked at Luke and met his gaze for a moment too long. She dragged her eyes away to the salad. "I can't cook, but I can toss a salad." Leah rounded the kitchen island and picked up the utensils. "What smells so good?"

"Lasagna."

"Yum."

Instead of a reply he picked up a beer and drank from it.

She looked up and noticed both Tobias and Taylor had disappeared.

Great.

HER HAND TREMBLED when she reached for her wine

glass. "Thank you for asking your brother to check on me."

"I wanted him to go sooner." He walked to the oven and opened it to peer in. "Wasn't sure if you'd left town."

Interesting that he'd yet to stop moving, didn't seem able to be still. Leah wasn't about to presume he was nervous around her. Nonetheless, the thought of it made her smile. "I thought about it. About leaving. It won't surprise anyone back in Billings."

He walked up to her, standing too close. "Not one to give up are you?"

Leah shook her head. "Its not just that. I don't have anything to go back to."

When she lifted her face up to look at him, his mouth crashed over hers. She grabbed at his shirt and pushed him against the counter. He was so large, so hard, a steady anchor in the center of tornado force winds. Strong arms surrounded her and his hands cupped her ass and lifted her off the floor.

Luke was a addicting elixir, the perfect combination of pleasure and risk.

When he dropped his hands and she stumbled backward, both stared at each other, chests heaving.

He turned away and grabbed his beer, his broad back providing enough cover as Taylor strolled in followed by Toby. Neither seemed to notice anything amiss as they were busy arguing over something Leah couldn't concentrate on enough to figure out.

She plastered a smile on and looked at Luke one

hand on the salad bowl. "Do you prefer it on the table or here?" She slid her hand over the kitchen island surface.

His gaze followed her hand. "Either is fine with me."

"Yeah Luke takes it where he can get it," Taylor quipped, laughing. He sobered when Toby elbowed him. "Sorry."

"Not a problem," Leah replied. "I did leave myself wide open."

The men all looked to each other and finally Leah held up both hands. "I did it again. Let's just eat before I say something else."

Thankfully the conversation was kept neutral over the meal. Leah was surprised at how helpful Tobias and Taylor were in giving her advice about how to turn her ranch into a profitable business. She ended up asking for a tablet and taking notes. Throughout the meal, Luke was quiet. His gaze constantly moved to her, and each time she squirmed in her seat.

Surely she'd lost her mind. How could she possibly want him so badly? He was trouble, unstable for starters. As far as she knew, he didn't even have a job. None of it mattered because her body craved him and by the way he looked at her, Luke knew it.

"I'll take you home." Luke stood. "Let me get the truck keys."

When he walked out, Tobias looked at her. "If he makes you uncomfortable, I can take you."

"I'm fine." She attempted to smile, but sighed instead. "Besides you two have plans. No worries, it's not that far."

CHAPTER SIXTEEN

THEY WERE GOING to have sex unless she got sense in her head and put a stop to it before reaching her house. Leah looked across the darkened interior of the truck. Luke kept his gaze straight ahead.

"You don't have to…"

"I want to."

With a long breath, she waited until he opened her door and stepped out of the truck. The night sky was blanketed with stars. She never got tired of looking up at it.

Luke stood next to her looking up. "When I was over there, I would stare at the sky at night and imagine I was here. Sometimes it would be the only thing that kept me from losing it."

"It's so beautiful. Makes me feel so insignificant."

He didn't reply, instead took her hand and brought it to his lips sending a tremble down the length of it.

When she tugged him in the direction of the house, he met her gaze. "Are you sure?"

"It doesn't make sense. I don't want to talk about it. Come inside please."

THE LIVING ROOM'S only light came from a small lamp on a side table. Shadows of tree branches cast by moonlight stretched across the flooring.

Luke grabbed Leah around the waist and pulled her against him, his mouth searching for hers as she slid her hands under his shirt. The muscles twitched under her palms as she ran her hands over the feathering of hair down the center of his chest.

She paused at his buckle and fumbled with it until unfastening it. He remained still allowing her to set the pace as she unbuttoned the fly.

With his help, she was able to push his pants and boxer briefs off his hips to free his erection.

He was already hard, so very hard.

Leah lowered to her knees while stroking him, her eyes locked to his. She took the tip of him into her mouth and swirled her tongue around it slowly, giving them both time to catch their breath.

When she cupped his sack and ran her pointed tongue down the underside of his sex, Luke's sharp inhalation was loud.

"Fuck yeah." His fingers slid through her hair, waiting for her to open her mouth. When she did, he drove past her lips.

Sucking the whole time, she took each inch of him

into her mouth while stroking him over and over.

Luke cupped her face and continued thrusting into her mouth each time deep until hitting the back of her throat. She held his hips managing to keep the pace although her eyes watered from the exertion.

Long moments later, when Leah put both hands on his hips, a silent signal to stop, Luke immediately pulled out.

His wide chest lifted and lowered with fast breathing as he helped her up to her feet.

This time he didn't have to command it. She undressed with shaky hands, her legs weakened with need, which made it hard to be graceful.

Fully naked, she stood in the moonlight and waited.

And then Luke shocked her.

Gloriously naked, he lowered to the rug and stretched out with his arms above his head.

It was up to her to follow through, to take it as far as she wanted. Of course he expected her to be afraid of him and a part of her was definitely not fully at ease. No matter what, she'd seen first hand how easily he could lose control. The wildness of him, the untamed man called to her innermost core.

Whether the excitement came from having him momentarily or the possibility of taming someone so untamable, she wasn't sure. But Luke Hamilton was one man she'd have a hard time letting go.

Leah straddled him and ran her hands down his chest. Leaning over, she took his proffered mouth and then followed by pressing kisses down the side of his jaw to his ear. When she reached his ear, his breathing had become jagged.

"I want you so bad right now," Leah whispered. "I want to fuck you Luke."

She reached between his legs, he was hard and ready. "You want me too." It was a statement, not a question.

After a long release of breath, he took her by the shoulders and pulled her against him.

While kissing her, he rolled Leah to the side. His mouth moved to her breasts while he slid his hand between her legs stroking and circling her nub with his finger tips until she cried out as the first climax hit.

When he slid down her body to take her into his mouth, he turned his body to give Leah access to his as well.

While he tasted and licked, she greedily sucked at his sex, enjoying the sounds of enjoyment both made.

"Shit," Luke pulled back. "Give me a minute." Puffing out air he rolled to his back.

"Are you all right?" Leah crawled up to lie beside him and studied his face.

A corner of his mouth lifted just a bit. "I got a cramp."

"Oh." Leah couldn't help but chuckle. "So you are human."

"Sometimes." He rolled over her and before long they became lost in each other again.

"WHAT TIME IS it?" Luke asked, buttoning up his shirt. It was hard to read his expression in the dim light, so Leah didn't bother.

She trudged to the kitchen and popped a coffee pod into the machine and placed a mug under it. "Nine-thirty, it's still early."

Torn between asking him to stay and hang out or pushing him out the door, she opted for humor. "So that was nice."

He didn't respond, instead turned to look out the window as lights flickered through it. "Someone's coming. Expecting company?"

Heart thudding, she hurried to the front windows and peered out. Of course being so dark outside, she couldn't see much more than the vehicle's headlights. "No. I'm not." She turned to him. "Do you mind waiting a bit, just until I see who that is?"

"Not at all." He remained standing, making the wait awkward.

"Want some coffee?"

"I'm good."

Finally the vehicle stopped and she watched as a familiar man climbed out. Her ex-husband, Gary, stared at Luke's truck before turning to the house.

"Shit. Great." Leah looked up at the ceiling and then to Luke. "It's okay. No need to stay."

Without a word they walked out through the door together. Luke walked down the stairs and straight to his truck without bothering to even acknowledge Gary's presence.

Gary on the other hand, followed Luke to the truck. "Who are you? What are you doing here?"

When Luke turned to him slowly, alarm bells rang in Leah's head. Hopefully Gary wouldn't do something stupid and provoke a reaction. She hurried to her ex.

"It's none of your business who my friend is. What are you doing here?"

Very slowly Gary pulled his gaze away from Luke, who finally got into the truck. Once he settled into the drivers' seat, Luke continued watching as if to make sure she wasn't in any trouble.

"I came to talk. But it seems you've been entertaining." Gary glared toward Luke. "Who the fuck is he?"

It was best to intercede and keep from any drama or worse. "He's my neighbor."

Gary didn't seem convinced but shrugged and finally walked toward the front door.

Leah lifted a hand to say goodbye to Luke. The cowboy started the truck blinding her with its lights. What the hell was it with men? It's not like she owed either of the assholes any kind of explanation. Especially not Gary, who'd cheated on her not once, but twice. That she knew of anyway.

Walking in front of her ex, Leah returned to the coffeemaker and grabbed her cup. Too annoyed to offer him one, she went about adding sugar and milk to it. "What do you want to talk about? Next time please call me first, don't just show up."

"Would I have interrupted something if I'd showed up earlier?" Gary walked around the front room looking around as if hunting for clues.

She gave him a droll look.

"I came to discuss our divorce agreement. I want to renegotiate the settlement of our house. You make enough money you don't need to get half of the sales profit. You're just doing it to get back at me for what happened. Before going to the lawyers and having you blindsided, I thought talking in person would be a better option."

Afraid she'd throw the hot coffee at him, she lowered the cup to the counter and glared at the idiot who waited with a bored expression.

"I allowed you to continue to live in the house and complete any needed repairs in exchange for us splitting the profit when we sold it. The house goes up for sale and now you want to renegotiate? How interesting." Leah lifted the cup to her lips and sipped the now tepid liquid.

Gary let out a huff. "Look, I am not here to fight."

"Then get the fuck out, because if you think I'm going to agree to you keeping all the money, you've lost your damn mind."

"Why do you have to be such a bitch," Gary said through gritted teeth. "You make way more money than I do…"

Leah had heard enough. They'd had the same argument over each piece of property from the cars to a damn boat she'd not wanted to buy in the first place. "You're wasting your time with this discussion. You have no idea what my income is and it's no longer any of your business. I'm tired of this song and dance. Have your lawyer contact mine." She rushed to the door and yanked it open. "I'm not an idiot. I know the property values have risen and the house is worth a lot more than we paid for it. So unless you want me to push the infidelity issue and line some pockets to screw you over like you deserve, I suggest you drop this. You'll get half, which is way more than a dog like you should get." She motioned to the outside with her head. "Leave now, or I'll call the police."

"I can't believe I married you."

"I can't believe you're here asking for money after screwing every thing that walks."

"You're a bitch."

"Yes I am. You're an idiot."

He stormed to his car and started it. When he put it in gear, the vehicle jerked forward before Gary realized he'd not put it in reverse. The loud grinding of gears made Leah grimace.

Watching her ex disappear into the night, she let out a sigh and leaned on the doorjamb.

What a night.

She looked up to the starry sky and immediately her thoughts went back to making love with Luke. Their lovemaking had been amazing, a slow race to completion and loss of control. He'd brought her to climax twice before taking his. Unlike the first time, this time had been different. He'd seemed more caring, almost as if he...

"Time to go to bed and stop being stupid," Leah said out loud, walking inside and locking the door. The last thing she needed to do was romanticize anything between her and Luke.

It had been sex, pure and simple, nothing else.

CHAPTER SEVENTEEN

"W HO PISSED IN your Wheaties this morning?" Taylor asked from across the table. "All I'm asking is if you'll go look at the cattle they're selling. It's not like you have anything else to do."

So obviously since he was the one without a job, he was sent to do stupid shit. In the case of Toby and Taylor, it meant they could boss him around and throw shit work at him. "I said I'd go."

"Look if you don't want to, I'll go tomorrow. I have contractors coming sometime today and the buyer for the horses will be here this afternoon."

It was obvious by Taylor's tone, his cousin was pissed about something. Usually it was hard to tell at which point Taylor lost his temper because the guy was a master of walking away.

Taylor looked down into his coffee. "I'm fucking tired man. I need time off." Piss in the Wheaties seemed to be the thing that morning.

"No one's stopping you. I can help out. Stop whining…damn." Luke looked up at the ceiling willing Taylor to just leave the kitchen.

"Who is she?"

"What?" Luke scratched at his beard. "Who are you talking about?"

Taylor shrugged, his wide shoulders lifting and lowering. "Got a hunch a woman is what's crawled up your ass. You've been an ass since the other night. Did you and Leah get into a fight or something?"

"Some guy came there when I was leaving. Seemed like an asshole."

Yeah, so that wasn't any kind of explanation. It was best to throw Taylor off and not make him think anything happened between him and Leah. It was a one-time…two-time thing, nothing else. She'd leave soon and other than some kind of accidental run in, he'd probably not see her ever again.

"What'd he look like? Older than us? About fifty? Kinda skinny?"

"Yeah."

"That's probably Gary, her ex. I met him a couple of years back when they were still married. He's a weasel."

Luke shrugged. Yeah he'd been 'that guy' and had waited up the road to see if the guy would stay. The ex had left less than fifteen minutes after getting there. By how fast he'd sped by, they'd not exactly had a good conversation. Luke had almost laughed. Leah could be a mean one when she put her mind to it. But under the flawless veneer and persona of a distant aloof woman was a softer, kind woman, who's laughter was musical and boy was she good in bed.

"… should have a few we can buy. The guy loves to haggle, so offer low to start."

Obviously Taylor had mistaken his silence for listening. Luke leaned forward putting his elbows on the table. "What time does the auction start? I'll get there early."

EVEN BEFORE SHE spoke, Luke could tell he was about to get ripped in to. Fire blazed from Leah's sharp gaze as she rushed to him. In a polo shirt and khakis, she didn't exactly look the part of a rancher, but her expression would keep anyone from stating so.

"You asshole. You stole those cows from under me." She pointed into the center of his chest. "Did you have to get those?"

He tried not to lose his temper. Of all the accusations, it was ridiculous that he'd have done anything of the sort on purpose. "I outbid everyone, I didn't know you were one of the bidders."

"Like hell you didn't, you looked right at me." She blinked back angry tears and turned on her heel.

A rancher he recognized walked up to him. "Good luck making up with your girlfriend, she looks pretty pissed."

"Not sure why she's mad at me, I wasn't the only one bidding against her."

The guy's eyebrows rose. "I reckon cause you and her... ya know."

Luke frowned. "What are you talking about? How would you know what we are to each other?"

"Sat right behind you. Thought she kept looking at me, but then saw how she watched you the whole time. It's obvious there's a thing between you and her."

Who was this clown, some sort of Hallmark movie character?

The man walked away whistling and Luke looked to where an angry Leah was talking to one of the brokers, her arms waving. Damn if she didn't look cute as all get out. Not that he'd ever be allowed near her again.

Luke went to where she argued with a man who stood outside the pen where the good-looking cows he'd bought were. The red heifers seemed to watch the argument, their large eyes focused on Leah.

"You told me they were mine and then you went and sold them out from under me without letting me know."

"Ma'am I'm not going to argue with you. Obviously, you're not aware of how things work around here..." The poor guy looked to Luke for help. "Tell her."

Leah swung to him and Luke managed to keep a blank look on his face. Barely.

"Don't talk to me Luke. I know exactly how things work. Since I don't have a dick between my legs, I'm instantly out."

The guy held his hands up in surrender. "Like I said. I'm not arguing. The deal has been made, money exchanged." The man walked backwards and then turned on his heel and hurried away.

"What do you want?" Leah seemed to be running out of steam, but he wasn't about to underestimate her.

"Making sure you're okay."

The sound she made was something between a groan and a wail. "Seriously? Luke, I swear if you don't step back, I'm going to hit you." She stomped her right foot and stormed away.

THE DRIVE TO Laurel Creek was slow as he trailered the cattle back. Half a dozen prized breeders and a bull. It would be a good start to a new herd. He'd purchased them for himself as he planned to stay there in Montana.

He'd not purchased the cows Taylor had wanted. He'd lost the bid on those. Taylor would have to haggle with the rancher on his own.

The long drive gave him time to think and consider what to do. He was tired of a pointless life, of days and nights in different towns. One of the things Doctor Sullivan had made him realize was that he needed to settle and put down some roots.

Hell at forty-five, he wondered if a rambler like him could do it. Settle down to what? Cows and land he supposed were a good start.

He pushed call on his phone and his father's voice came over the speaker. "Hey boy, you all right?"

"Bought some cows and a bull today. I want to go

ahead and build something. Set up a home on the land."

There was a long silence and he wondered if his Dad was about to hang up. Although he'd never meant to hurt him, Luke knew his father didn't trust him anymore.

"I'm glad to hear it. You sound different. I really want to believe you'll stay, cause its time son. You're not going to bring those boys back by blaming yourself you know?"

Luke swallowed past the lump forming in his throat. "I know…"

"Look. You know what part of the land is yours. Keep your little herd on Taylor's land for now until you build something. Make sure you get a sturdy pen for the bull." His father was enjoying giving him instructions and the sound of his voice slowly overtook the others that told him he didn't deserve it, none of it. Shouldn't plan for a future when he'd stolen theirs.

Deep down inside Luke knew beating himself up and not allowing for a good life wouldn't help anyone, least of all the guys who'd died. But every single time he'd tried, the ending had been the same.

No, he didn't blame fate, or bad luck, for failing so many times. It was all him. Luke was the master of self-sabotage.

"We expect you for dinner on Sunday," his father said not leaving room for arguments.

Dust from the road flew up as a gust of wind swept across it. A bird flew across too close to the windshield and he couldn't hit the brakes, not with a trailer behind him. The damn thing barely missed getting hit.

Luke's breath caught and his vision blurred.

"Down to single digits Sarg," O'Brien said with a wide grin. "Can't wait to sink my teeth into a real burger. Wash it down with a cold beer."

Despite the sweltering heat combined with sand that managed to get into every crevice as they rode in the Humvee, the kid's disposition rarely changed. Even on patrol, when walking in silence, O'Brien would look over and wink at a new soldier or flash his smile at another one who was scared shitless and on the verge of tears.

The loud boom came out of nowhere. One minute they were on the ground, the next Luke flew several feet from the vehicle and banged his head so hard he saw stars. Ears ringing, he half dragged, half crawled back to the smoking vehicle.

One soldier remained slumped over in the seat. He yanked the door open and dragged him to the side of the road, not bothering to check his pulse. He had to get to O'Brien... the kid was going home.

Heart thumping so loud it echoed in his dulled ears, Luke made his way back stumbling and falling hard onto the ground when his left leg gave out.

It was a struggle to get back up, but finally he hurried past another soldier who was obviously dead by the unfocused look of his gaze and found O'Brien. He'd been blown farther. He noticed his legs first ...one completely gone from the knee down, the other at an odd twisted angle.

"Hang on. You're fine, you're going to be okay." Luke didn't want to chance dragging him, but the fire under the Humvee worried him.

"I'm going to move you kid, this is going to hurt," he croaked out meeting the young guy's dull gaze.

Through the blood and sand, O'Brien's gaze met his for a long moment. "I'm not gonna make it Sarg."

A second explosion sounded and Luke fell over O'Brien. He had to protect the kid. He was down to single-digits…less than ten days.

The rumble of driving too close to the edge of the road brought Luke back to the present, just barely.

His lungs protested his lack of breathing and Luke shook his head in a futile attempt to clear his vision. Scared shitless he'd roll the trailer, Luke slowed and pulled over. His hands shook as he exited the truck and bent at the waist blowing out air in an attempt to keep from throwing up. A viselike grip around his chest grew so tight he fell to his knees. Damn, if he was having a heart attack, this would be the place that guaranteed death.

He'd not seen another car for at least an hour.

These were the classic signs of a panic attack he decided, as his breathing finally slowed and the vice loosened. He let out long breaths, climbed back into the truck and fell back against the headrest.

Doctor Sullivan had instructed him on how to deal with these episodes, how to mentally work through them. It sounded silly to even try, but he did. Slowly at first he repeated the phrase to himself, and then again out loud.

"I am here for a reason. I matter. I matter."

A tear slid down his cheek and he stared at the open land spread out as far as the eye could see. Montana was beautiful and damn it, it would be where he started living again.

"I deserve happiness. I am worth it. I matter." Once again he repeated the words out loud, and as the tightness finally lifted, he slumped over the steering wheel and wept.

CHAPTER EIGHTEEN

C LACK. CLACK. CLACK. Had her heels always
sounded like that? Every step toward her office
made her want to run in the opposite direction. In a
pantsuit and black heels, her hair up in a French twist,
Leah was back in her element. At least that's what she
kept repeating to herself.

The meeting was important, the client was one of
hers. Although ostracized from the company, they
needed her there for one of the company's most lucrative
accounts. One she'd worked hard for months to acquire.

She'd been reviewing the files from the ranch and
had spoken to the man several times. To the client, there
wouldn't be any indication she was not working directly
for him.

At the last moment, Leah turned away from her
office and instead went to her father's.

The walk past the people she'd worked with for ten
years made her heart speed up. To her surprise, the
junior personnel pretended as if she'd just been there the

day before throwing out a "Hey Leah" and a "Good morning".

The lingering looks blanketed her back as she moved to where her father's administrative assistant looked up with a warm smile. Unlike the rest of the staff, Ellen didn't pretend everything was the same. "Hello Sweetheart, I've missed you." The woman rounded her desk and hugged her. "I hope this is the beginning of your return," she whispered in Leah's ear, voicing the opinion that told her, Ellen had not agreed with her father.

"Thank you," Leah replied hugging her back. "I missed you too."

"Go on in." Ellen motioned to her father's open door. "I'm sure he's expecting you."

Patrick Morgan did not look his age. Despite long hours while heading Morgan Investments, one of the largest investment companies in Montana, he remained mostly devoid of gray hair, except for his temples.

At sixty-seven, most would be considering retirement. Although he did take regular vacations mostly to appease her mother, who loved to travel, he didn't seem to have immediate plans to leave the workforce.

"Settled in for the week?" He met her gaze without smiling. This was the CEO who spoke to her, not her father. "I need to go over some details with you and Zack at nine-thirty."

His phone rang and he ignored it. "Sit down, need to go over some recent changes to the Lawhead account with you now."

It was as if nothing had changed. Nothing other than she wasn't truly a member of the workforce. A part of her felt detached as hurt formed a barrier protecting Leah from hoping she'd be allowed to return permanently.

Half an hour later in the conference room, Leah along with the executives sat at a long table. The discussion went unabated as each person presented their current stats and such. Leah wouldn't have any input. Other than being there to represent the company to the client, she was devoid of responsibility.

Her gaze moved to the window. The street view of another building across the parking lot was not exactly what one would call picturesque. The views at the ranch were so much better. At the moment, she yearned to be back there, in the security of the empty house.

At the same time, what did she have there? No friends. Any attempts at prospering the ranch were feeble at best. She needed direction, needed to know exactly what she wanted.

For goodness sakes, she was forty-two years old.

What did she want?

"Care to join us Leah?" Her father's voice brought her out of her revelry.

"Unless it's about the Lawhead account, we all know my presence or opinion doesn't really matter at the moment."

There was an awkward silence as everyone looked anywhere but at her or her father.

"Need you to go over two portfolios sometime after

the meeting with Lawhead and his people."

She nodded and looked across the table at Zack, her father's right hand man. The guy had the audacity to smile at her. He seemed pale and thinner, or had he always been like that?

He paled in comparison to Luke.

Shit the last thing she needed to think about was Luke Hamilton. The man had proven to be the asshole she thought he was on the first day they'd met.

WHAT SEEMED LIKE an eternity later, Leah leaned back in her office chair and closed her eyes. It was almost seven in the evening and they'd finally finished for the day. How had she done it for so long? Working twelve to fourteen hour days then slogging home to take out or a sandwich. Most days she'd popped open her laptop and continued working until bedtime.

Yet she'd been happy, or content at least.

"It's not the same without you here." Zack stood in the doorway.

"Says the man who has the most to gain by my absence." Leah couldn't keep the disdain from her voice. "I doubt you miss me."

Zack had the decency to look chagrined. Of course he'd tried to convince her father against her being sent away. What better way to gain the trust of the CEO and get her to believe he was the nice guy?

It wasn't until now, she could see the gleam of

shrewdness in his gaze. There had always been something about him that seemed off. At times she'd considered that perhaps she was attracted to him, which could be why a sort of apprehension took over when he was in the room.

The distance, having been gone for several weeks, helped her see clearer. He was not a nice man, not about what was best for others. Zack was a schemer, who was positioning himself for power. The only way to get her father to agree would be if she seemed unfit. Although, she had to admit, he was good at his job. Very good.

Her eyes narrowed. "Why am I really here? Please don't tell me it was your idea for me to be present."

He stepped into her office but didn't sit. Of course not, he preferred to stand over her. "It's your account after all. You had to be here." Lowering to place his hands flat on her desk, he leaned closer. "Why do you have such a problem with me all of a sudden? All I've done was try to help, when the others asked that you be fired." He shook his head. "You need to work on your trust issues. I'm not the enemy here."

Oh it could be her husband screwed around on her, her former lover had screwed her out of a deal and her father was being swayed against her by a schemer, or maybe the fact that the schemer himself was now trying to act like her friend? She had a lot of reasons to not trust the opposite sex.

"Zack, I'm not going to be psychoanalyzed by you. How about we call it a day?"

"How about a celebratory drink? Give me a break, I'm trying to be friends with you."

If she closed her eyes, maybe when she opened them, he'd be gone. Leah tried and it didn't work. He remained leaning over her desk with a perfected 'I'm a nice guy' expression. Lips curved, eyes hooded and eyebrows lifted, Zack peered down at her.

"Well, it's nice to see my two favorite people are getting along." Her father picked the worst moment possible to stroll in. As his gaze moved from Zack to her, his wide smile made Leah want to scream.

"I was just asking your daughter out for a celebratory drink," Zack, the asshat, announced. "Would you like to join us?"

"Perfect idea," her father replied and then looked at her. "Your mom is spending the week at your brother's. She's watching the kids while they go on a cruise."

It was hard not to cringe. Her brother could have asked her. But then again, she'd not been to see her nieces in several months. Not wishing to have any family conversation in front of Zack, she stood and grabbed her purse and work tote. "Let's go have a drink."

IT WAS ALMOST eleven at night, when Leah finally trudged home. The condo was pristine as always. The lighting was purposely bright in some areas and dimmer in others to create a welcoming environment.

Decorated in shades of pale gray and white, although

beautiful, it now seemed sterile. She kicked off her shoes and dropped her bags onto a chair on her way to the bedroom.

In the center of her bed was a box, and she stopped in her tracks looking around. Who could have possibly come into the place? Beside her parents, only Allison had a key.

She tiptoed to the bed, as if the box would come to life and attack her. Gently, she untied the satiny Tiffany blue ribbon, which slipped from her fingers to the bedding, the color adding a touch of brightness to her stark white coverlet.

Inside the box, a small dried flower wreath sat nestled in white tissue. In the center was a note card with the Pollyanna logo.

> I know it was a hard day.
>
> Lets do lunch tomorrow.
>
> Hugs, Alli

If she didn't already love her friend, now she did more. Tears stung as Leah sat on the bed. She lifted the beautiful little wreath and sniffed it. It smelled of lavender, reminding her of Allison's flower shop.

After a quick text to her friend setting a time and place, she hurried to shower. Within moments she was settled in bed, her eyes barely remaining open.

"HOLY COW!" ALLISON'S wide eyes met hers. "Twice.

And wow…"

"Yes, it was stupid."

Allison leaned closer and whispered even though they were the only ones in the flower shop at the time. "If a man made me come that many times and so hard, I would sleep with him more than twice."

"He's trouble. Has issues. Besides, like I said, the asshole outbid me on purpose."

"I'm sure that's not the case."

Leah shook her head. "He was staring at me the entire time."

"Maybe because you're lovers. Hello?" Allison tapped the side of her own head. "Plus, it doesn't matter, you've got it bad for him."

"No I don't. The sex was great, but that's all it was. It's over."

"No it's not."

Why had she admitted to her friend what happened with Luke? She had to change the topic. The last thing she needed was Luke constantly on the brain. "What's new with you? Have you had mindblowing sex lately?" Okay how was that changing the topic?

"Not like you apparently," Allison said, laughing. "The man can cook, is great in bed, and on top of that he's hot. I can't imagine him naked. Woo!" She fanned her face. "Hot and a good lover. Girl, do you know how hard it is to find guys our age like that?"

"We're not that old. Forties is the new thirty." Leah couldn't keep from smirking at the cliché.

"For women maybe, but the guys didn't get the memo. Luke is forty-five and he can go for that long. That alone would make me forget any assholishness."

A burst of laughter escaped and Leah was so glad she could come and spill her guts to her dear friend. "God, I love you. You always make me forget my troubles."

Allison took her right hand in both of hers. "Stop it. You don't have troubles. You are on sabbatical. You are beautiful. Think about it. How many women get a chance to get away to a ranch for six months? No responsibility. Can lie around all day and read. Ride horses, explore, paint or some other stupid hobby. You have money so you don't have to worry too much. On top of that, you have a hot lover…kinda. If you complain one more time, I'm going to have to bitch-slap you."

"Holy shit. You just made my life sound amazing." Leah pretended to be shocked. Shame edged in. "Geez, you're right. I need to get my head out of my ass."

"You think?"

The bell over the door jingled and both looked up as a woman bustled in. Cheeks flushed, she returned Allison's greeting. "Hi I'm picking up flowers for the Clark wedding."

"Hello Mrs. Stanley." Allison led the woman to a beautiful upholstered chair. "Have a cup of tea, while I finish boxing the flowers. It won't take but a second." She quickly poured tea and placed it in the befuddled woman's hands. "There's a choice of honey or raw sugar." She pointed to a small tray on the side table next to the woman's elbow. As Allison glided to the back room, a soft harp musical began playing.

Mrs. Stanley lifted the tea to her lips. In less than a minute, the woman's shoulders fell and she let out a long breath. As if noticing Leah for the first time, she smiled in her direction. "I needed this break. I'm the mother of a very demanding bride."

Leah smiled in return.

CHAPTER NINETEEN

"I'M TOO OLD for this shit." Luke let out a huff and dropped into a chair. The kids he'd been chasing continued running circles in the back yard. Family dinners were great, but his younger sister seemed to always have more kids each time he visited and the little buggers were relentless.

His sister was the youngest of the three of them. Currently twenty-eight, she'd gotten married at nineteen to her high school sweetheart after finding out she was pregnant. The couple was well suited and now ten years later had four kids.

Taylor laughed and also collapsed into a chair on the back patio. "Yeah, they're a handful." Although his cousin seemed to enjoy the day, Luke knew it had to be hard for him.

After the entire horrible event of his father's death, Taylor's in-laws were killed in a tragic accident. In the car with them were both his five-year-old son and toddler-aged daughter.

Although the entire family had mourned the great loss, Luke couldn't imagine how much harder it was for Taylor. To top it off, Taylor and his wife divorced soon after, the marriage unable to withstand so much loss.

"Thanks for letting me pen my cows with yours." Luke took a long drink of his lemonade. "I am still figuring out what kind of house to build."

Taylor laughed. "You've got a great piece of land, can build pretty much anything on it."

"Yeah," he replied shaking his head. "Dad still takes good care of us."

"Yep," Taylor agreed. "I'm not sure what I'd do without them."

"I'm right there with you," Luke replied.

His mother walked out. In a long sleeveless dress, with her hair swept up into a twist of some sort, she looked much younger than sixty-two. "How are my boys?" She cupped Taylor's jaw before turning to Luke. "You look great, relaxed. Montana is doing you good sweetheart."

He couldn't help the smile. "You are beautiful as always Mom."

She chuckled. "You're sweet." Her gaze moved to the back yard. "Kids, dinner is ready. Come on." The children ran to her and she guided them inside. "Come in boys, let's eat."

TOBIAS DROVE THEM back from their parents'. Luke

leaned back in the front passenger seat, too full to be comfortable.

"So what happened the other day? You said you felt sick." Tobias glanced toward him.

"I am not sure what the hell that was," Luke explained to Tobias who studied his face. "Pretty sure it was some kind of panic attack. I'm good now."

His brother didn't seem convinced. "I still think we should get you checked out. If it's your ticker, best to know."

"I'm good." The last thing he needed was to spend hours at some doctor's office. He was already seeing the psychiatrist, which was more than enough.

Tobias grinned. "I'll tell Mom if you don't go."

Luke groaned.

In the back seat Taylor snored and jerked awake. "What happened?"

"Looks like Miss Pesky is back," Tobias said looking toward the Morgan land. "She's something else. I heard about what happened at the auction. Heard she had a fit."

"I outbid her and she took it personally. Didn't even know I was bidding against her, there were others bidding too." Luke watched the house as they drove past. The lights were on in every room. On the side of the house her small car was parked at an angle.

"She could have talked to the guy and arranged for a separate purchase. Instead, I think she probably scared the crap out of him." Tobias chuckled.

Luke laughed. "Yeah, she most definitely did."

"So what's going on with you two?" Taylor was the one brave enough to ask.

Luke wondered how much he and Tobias suspected to have transpired. He shrugged. "She hates me. That's about it."

"Mmm. Hmm," Tobias said not taking his eyes from the road.

They arrived at the house, which gave him a reprieve from more questions.

"Shit." Leah ducked into a doorway at spotting Luke standing in front of the hardware store where a man and his wife had dogs in small pens and on leashes. She'd come to town to see about the dogs, which had been on the news the night before. Seemed the couple took it upon themselves to run a no-kill shelter.

He didn't seem the kind to want or need a dog. They already had two at their house. She peeked out and sure enough, he'd crouched down to the dogs' level. It was best to give him some time and then come back. She hurried to a coffee shop just a couple of doors down.

"Nice day isn't it?" the woman behind the counter greeted her. "What can I get for you?"

After ordering a latte and a bagel, she found a table where she could keep an eye out toward where the dogs were. Once Luke left, she'd go over and see the dogs. Although she wanted one, she'd not owned one since leaving home.

Now it seemed would be the perfect time to train a dog and spend time with it before going back to live in Billings. She considered her condo and how hard it would be for an animal to go from a ranch to living in a restricted space.

She glanced out the window toward where the dogs were and Luke wasn't there. Leah leaned forward and scanned the street. Had he picked out a dog and left already?

"Leah." His deep voice sunk in and her treacherous stomach tumbled. "Saw you outside."

Damn, had he seen her hiding in the doorway? "Yeah, I saw you too." She looked up at him with a blank expression. There was no way she was about to start a conversation with him.

"The usual?" the woman called from behind the counter and he turned to give her a nod. "Thank you."

He had a "usual"?

Thankfully he left and went to get his "usual". But her relief was short lived when he returned and lowered into the empty seat opposite her. His hazel eyes met hers and she let out a breath. "Why are you sitting here? There are plenty of empty chairs." She motioned to the otherwise empty café.

Just then a group of four women entered. Chatting loudly, they ordered drinks while maintaining an ongoing conversation. The woman who owned the shop was obviously their mutual friend.

"You're still mad at me?"

He was playing with her now. Although his expression was hard to read, she wondered if he really gave a shit. "Of course I am. You know that was wrong."

"You can negotiate with Barrett about more animals. He will work with you."

"Did you hear what they said? That was the last set he's offering for a couple years."

He leaned closer. "They always say things like that to get people to bid."

From his eyes, she trailed her gaze down to his lips. It took monumental willpower to look away and out the window. "Are you getting a dog?"

"Can I come over tonight?"

"No."

"I'm not sure about the dog. You?"

Now that she thought about it, perhaps getting a dog was impulsive. "I'm not sure."

"It would be good protection."

When he lifted the coffee to his mouth, she was able to look back to him. "I am not staying in Laurel Creek forever. Once I leave, the dog would have to adjust to living in a condo with a microscopic yard."

He seemed to ponder her words. "How about you? Will you have a hard time adjusting to being away?"

Of course he meant Laurel Creek, but all she could think of was not seeing him again. And how sitting there now across from him felt almost perfect. It was as if they had a real relationship, just then. He drank his coffee not seeming to mind the silence between them as she picked at her bagel.

"I did it before. Left Laurel Creek to go away to college. After that Dad asked that I begin working for him, so I went directly to Billings."

Luke studied her, his gaze moving across her face before he looked out the window. "They've got one you should meet."

She finished her bagel after giving him half and they walked out. Leah couldn't help the awareness of it when his hand pressed against the small of her back to guide her across the street.

Dogs barked at their nearing, a couple others wagged their tails and strained to reach them held back by leashes. One in particular, a tiny brown mixed-breed, gave high-pitched yaps and wagged its tail, its attention only on Luke.

"Seems like one's picked you out." It was comical to see the large guy try to put off the tiny dog who wouldn't stop trying to get his attention.

Leah laughed as she kneeled to pet a pretty black lab mix. The dog nudged at her hand with its head, inviting for more scratches behind the ears.

"She's so sweet," the woman told her. "It's hard to get black dogs adopted out, especially once they get older. Most people want the lighter and younger ones."

The dog seemed to smile at her, its eyes meeting hers. "How old is she?"

"About three. Sweet as can be," the woman said,

seeming encouraged by Leah's interaction with the dog.

"We named her Rosie, but if you take her, you can rename her."

"Why Rosie?"

The woman looked to her husband. "He named her that. She was dumped. A lady found her asleep in her rose garden."

"Oh." Leah looked at the dog, who's tail wagged furiously. "It suits her." She straightened and went to Luke who now held the tiny dog. "So which dog did you want to show me?"

Luke held out the tiny bundle. "This little guy."

Lifting the light dog, she tried to get its attention, but the dog kept its gaze on Luke. Leah let out a sigh and returned him to Luke. The little dog licked at his jaw happy to be returned.

"I think he's picked you out."

"What am I going to do with this hawk bait?" Luke placed it down and it sat next to his foot. "Can't take him. He's too little," he explained to the woman who looked between them. "We've only had him for a week. Hopefully someone will take him soon. He's cute."

Leah smiled at the woman. "I'll take Rosie."

AFTER A TRIP to the store to get dog food, leashes and a dog bed, Leah finally went back to the car to unload her things. She'd agreed to return to pick up the dog so she drove to where the couple were now packing up the remaining dogs.

Seemed as if they'd had a successful day. They had only three dogs left, so that meant they'd adopted out about six.

Leah hurried to Rosie who jumped up and down wagging her tail. Leah grinned like a loon and then smiled at the woman who handed her Rosie's leash. "Thank you. What happened to the little tiny dog? It got adopted?"

"Oh yes." The woman smiled broadly. "Your friend, the good looking man. He came back for him."

She'd figured that would happen once she left. Neither the little dog nor Luke could stop looking at each other.

With her very happy dog, she went back to the car. At once Rosie settled into the back seat seeming to know she was safe. The entire drive home, Leah kept looking to the back loving the site of the trust in Rosie's eyes.

The thought of being responsible for another's well being filled her with awe and she blinked back tears. How a bundle of fur could bring out so much protectiveness in her was crazy.

CHAPTER TWENTY

ROSIE BARKED AND Leah looked away from her book to the windows. Lights from an approaching vehicle shined through the glass panes. She didn't have to wonder who it was. What she didn't know was whether she'd let him in or not.

This couldn't continue. Sex with Luke was great, addictive even, but to what end?

She let out a breath. "I don't know Rosie. It's hard to say no lately it seems."

The dog whimpered and pawed at the front door probably hearing Luke's footsteps approaching.

Leah yanked the door open and stepped onto the porch. Rosie rushed past her to greet Luke.

He gave the dog attention before walking closer.

Not sure what to do other than wait, Leah crossed her arms not speaking.

His gaze moved from her to the door, the silent signal loud and clear.

"We're not having sex." Leah let out a breath and

tried to calm her thundering heart. She wanted to have sex. Was actually already undressing him in her mind. But this was not what she wanted. Not exactly sure what it was she wanted from Luke, but it was definitely more than just sex.

"Okay." He stood at the bottom of the steps.

"What do you want from me Luke?"

"Not sure." At least he was honest. Then again she'd just thought the same thing.

In the distance birds flew to nest for the night. The breeze was already turning chilly, signaling the coming of fall. She'd be there for months, spending time alone with just Rosie for company. It became clear what she wanted. Someone to spend time with, to do simple things like watch television or cook breakfast with.

She let out a fortifying huff. "I don't know how I feel about you Luke. I am mad at you. I am attracted to you. Sometimes I don't want to see you at all and other times I want nothing more."

Brows knitted he remained silent so she continued. "I do know things between us, the way they are, need to stop. We fight one minute and the next we're friends. I enjoy having sex with you, but I am looking for more than just that with you. And yes, I know I'm not making much sense right now."

LUKE WASN'T SURE what to say at the moment. Was he ready for a relationship? Could he set himself up for another disappointment? To let his guard down was something he wasn't sure he was able to handle. Putting trust in another person had not panned out well up to this point. Although he'd expected to be turned away, he didn't think she'd be so upfront about her feelings. He admired that in the woman, who looked at him now with expressive eyes. Your turn they said.

"Not sure what to say." Yeah that was a good come back. Sounded like some kind of idiot. Luke cleared his throat.

"I get it. That you prefer someone who will make assurances. Don't blame you." He shoved his hands into the front pockets of his jeans. He should leave. Unfortunately his feet and legs didn't get the memo and stayed planted. Luke wracked his brain for what to say. He wanted to see her, to get to know Leah. That was something wasn't it?

"Would you like to go out to eat?"

"When?" She looked to her dog as if the animal could give her advice.

He shrugged. "Tomorrow night?"

Other than Shooters, which he was banned from, there was the coffee shop, a small diner and a pizza joint in Laurel Creek. Not much more.

"Umm. Sure. Okay." Her lips lifted, probably at the awkwardness of the moment. "Pick me up at six?"

"Sounds good." He neared her. "Good night Leah."

She let out a breath. "Good night."

He didn't try anything as she seemed skittish. Instead

he leaned and patted the dog's head much to the animal's delight. "Not much of a guard dog are you?"

As he walked away to his truck, he could feel Leah's gaze following him. It was kind of nice to know she watched. His mouth curved into a smile but he quickly got rid of it before turning to wave as he climbed into the truck.

Six O'CLOCK SHARP the next day, he knocked on Leah's door. Inside the dog barked and its face appeared at the window. Tongue lolling to the side, it seemed to smile.

When his knock wasn't answered, he knocked again. Although he was sure the dog had more than alerted Leah that someone was there.

Did she plan to stand him up? Damn if he didn't feel stupid now. Luke took a step back, shocked at the tightness threatening around his chest.

Just then the door opened and Leah appeared. Her flushed face brightened at seeing him. "Sorry. I was in the bathroom. Nerves or something." She stepped back. "Come in. I'll get my purse."

He let out a breath taking her in fully. Dressed in black tight pants and a frilly off the shoulder black and white top, she looked amazing. Unfortunately all he could think of was taking the clothes off. "You look nice."

Leaning to pet the dog, she turned to look up at him. "Thank you." She turned back to her new pet. "Here's a huge bone, and a snack." She placed a rawhide bone and a couple of dog biscuits on the floor next to the dog's bed. "Be a good girl."

"I'm ready," she announced looking up at him and boy didn't that just send some kind of thing to his belly.

They walked out and Luke caught a whiff of her perfume. The fragrance was one she always wore and he could barely take his eyes away from the exposed skin of her shoulders. "How does pizza sound?"

She gave him a knowing look. "Perfect."

THEY FOUND AN empty table in the corner of the pizza restaurant. Luke sat with his back to the wall and she across from him in the small two-person space. His adam's apple bobbed and he let out shallow breaths. It was interesting how he seemed more nervous than her. Then again, he did have some sort of PTSD condition. Something she wanted to know more about before getting into any kind of relationship with him.

She'd talked to an excited Allison about her upcoming date and although her friend was enthusiastic at the prospect, she'd warned her to find out what steps he was taking to help with any flashbacks.

They ordered beer and a pizza to share, and once the drinks were served, Leah decided it was best to get the conversation going. "Can I ask you about your episodes? Do they happen often?"

He looked into his beer in thought. "I never apologized for that night. I know it scared you and Allison."

It shocked her that he remembered she and Allison were there. "It was scary. You seemed out of control."

He met her gaze. "I was court ordered to see a psychiatrist. I'll be honest, I've seen several. But this guy seems to get it. Teaching me different ways to cope."

"That's good." Leah drank from her beer waiting to see what else he'd say.

"As far as how often. I can't say. I've been good lately."

"You avoiding crowds and such though?"

"Other than the cattle auction, yes. Which is why I didn't know I was bidding against you. I did see you, but was concentrating on your face to stay sane with all the noise and such."

Leah blinked. She wasn't sure what to think. "You did?"

Luke nodded.

The server came with their pizza. The woman placed it between them and then slid plates in front of each before asking if they wanted refills.

The entire time, she couldn't look away from Luke. What happened? Why did he choose her? Why did she feel so compelled toward him?

God none of it made any sense. If anything, they were completely wrong for each other.

On so many levels.

CHAPTER TWENTY-ONE

O N THE DRIVE back to Leah's, tension was tangible, neither sure what the next step was. Luke glanced at her. "How do you like having a dog?"

Her shoulders lowered and she smiled. "Rosie is great. Although I feel a sense of responsibility like never before. It's funny, I don't mind it, plus it's nice to have the company." Cocking her head to the side, she studied him. "It's hard to picture you with the tiny dog you took. He really likes you."

"Not so much. The little traitor follows Taylor around more than me. As soon as we got home, he ensured the other dogs knew he was Alpha and then peed on my boot."

Her laughter was nice and he let it soak in.

The truck swayed left, the tires sinking into a hole. The jarring made Leah yelp as she bumped against the passenger door.

"Sorry, I wasn't paying attention." Luke gripped the steering wheel as the familiar ringing in his ears began.

"It's okay," Leah replied with a giggle. "I'll have to keep that pothole in mind. My car will end up in the shop if I don't avoid it." She continued but he couldn't hear anything other than the rush of blood past his ears and thudding of his heart.

He managed to keep it together long enough to get her home and on unsteady legs walked her to her door. After a hasty kiss that obviously left her startled, he rushed back to his truck.

Somehow he managed to sit long enough to watch her go inside before he threw the truck in reverse and hightailed it out of there.

He couldn't go into his house. The dogs, questions and lights would only make it worse.

So he parked near the stables and stumbled out of the truck.

The dimness of the interior and smell of hay would hopefully bring him back to realizing he wasn't there. He was home. Safe.

"Down to single digits Sarg," O'Brien's smiling face waivered in the darkness. "Can't wait to sink my teeth into a real burger. Wash it down with a cold beer."

Blood everywhere. Dust. The sun sizzling on his skin as he labored to breathe.

Luke tried to reach O'Brien, but his body didn't follow any signals.

Boom! A second explosion sounded and he scrambled into the darkness of a corner. Where was he? Where were his men?

Tears mixed with sweat as he trembled and fell to his side griping his legs. He curled into a ball as he tried to keep from screaming.

Thudding continued and he wasn't sure if it was in his head or outside.

"I hate you." His voice seemed to echo in his head as he spoke out loud. "Help me."

Luke wasn't sure how much time had passed. Sometime in the night, he'd fallen asleep and awoke when footsteps sounded.

"Luke?" Tobias called out. "You in here?"

"Yeah." He couldn't stop the shaking that took over as his brother's familiar face lowered.

"Hey Bud." Tobias lowered and sat next to him. Not touching him, but close enough his twin's body heat became a beacon of hope. "Wanna talk?"

"I'm fucking forty-five years old."

Tobias chuckled. "No shit? I didn't know that."

It was nice when he could finally take in a full breath without the constriction in his chest. "I don't need to be in anyone's life. Need to face reality."

"Everyone has issues. You don't get to corner the market on that."

Luke struggled to sit but his arms shook too hard. Tobias pulled him up and he fell back against the wall. His brother's arms around him helped the tightness to ease.

"This is more than issues." Luke squeezed his eyes shut when the overhead lights flashed on.

"What's going on?" Taylor rushed to them. "You hurting Luke?" His heavy palm landed on Luke's shoulder. "Can you talk?"

"Good thing you're not a paramedic," Luke grumbled, covering his face to avoid the glare of the bright lights. Horses nickered, also complaining.

"Turn the lights off dumbass," Tobias said chuckling. "The horses are going to think it's morning."

A moment later only dim lights remained on. His cousin stood looking down at him and Tobias. "What happened?"

"I lost my shit," Luke said, looking up at his cousin. "I'm good. Go on to bed. I'll crash here."

There was a beat of silence as Taylor and Tobias exchanged looks.

"Why don't we go inside? You can crash in your bedroom." His brother wouldn't let the subject drop and Luke didn't want to explain that he feared another flashback if he moved.

"I forgot what Doc told me to do. I couldn't do it." He stood up and blew out a breath. "So much for all that."

Tobias rolled his eyes. "So, you're giving up, just like that? Dude it's gonna take time."

Right, the one thing he didn't have. Not now. If he had any chance with Leah, it would be gone by the time he got better. Hell, what would have happened if he'd not been able to control it and had lost it while he was with her? She would have probably freaked out.

The three walked out of the stables. It wasn't lost on him that his brother and cousin flanked him ensuring to keep him in between.

"Orion." Tobias pointed at the night sky.

He followed suit and his lips curved. "Yeah, there he is."

Just before deploying, they'd made an agreement that when spotting Orion it meant the other was safe.

The constellation seemed to brighten and Luke could only think of the irony. Safe could mean so many things. Yes, he was safe, had been spared. The others that he'd ordered to join him on that patrol, not so much.

"Why do you think I'm here?" The words startled not just his companions, but him as well. He'd not even been thinking it.

Taylor let out a sigh. "Because some of us are lucky bastards. We get to hang out longer and do shit before our time is up."

How was it that although he'd lost so much, Taylor could always remain so optimistic? Although flashes of pain appeared on occasion, the guy never lost sight of what was important.

"Well said Cuz," Tobias said and looked to him. "What's your excuse for existing?"

"To kick your ass," Luke replied.

"That's not happenin'."

"I'll go see Doc tomorrow."

"That's good," both Tobias and Taylor spoke in unison.

THREE DAYS AND she'd not heard from Luke. A part of her wasn't surprised. The easiest way to get rid of a guy is to mention the "R" word. She'd told him she wanted more, a relationship.

Rosie ran off chasing something or other. Probably an invisible foe, since Leah couldn't make out anything in the distance. A man and woman, realtors finally emerged from the house. She'd purposely left them alone to take their time inspecting every room at their leisure.

Both assumed perfect professional smiles at nearing, but it didn't fool her. She was the master at reading what many considered a professional mask. They were interested, very much so.

"Ms. Morgan," the woman started as they'd devised a plan for her to be the first to speak and set up trust. "After riding over the acreage and now seeing the house, we are prepared to assist you with the sale of the property."

The man nodded, his perfect hair barely stirring in the breeze. "We can draw up a plan, I seriously doubt it will be on the market long. It's becoming very popular for younger couples to move out to the country. Farm style living is a movement right now."

She accepted their cards and turned over her shoulder to look for Rosie who'd yet to appear from where she'd run off.

The realtors left, but she didn't go with them to their

car, instead went to find Rosie. The dog lay on her back, her legs up in the air as she wiggled on the ground.

"Come Rosie," Leah said nearing only to back up at the putrid smell. "Oh my God."

The happy dog followed her back to the house as Leah tried to figure out how the hell she was going to wash the stupid dog. She'd have to find a water hose.

The man standing beside the house made her stomach dip until she realized it was Tobias. Funny how the identical twins caused such different reactions.

She waved.

"Hey, what's up neighbor?"

"Not much, saw some suits driving away as I was headed home. Making sure you're okay."

She looked in the direction of the road unsure of how much to share with him. "Yes, they are realtors. I've decided to sell the ranch. I'll stay here until it does. It's too much for me to handle alone."

"You know they'll divide it and sell it in parcels. Let me talk to my brother, maybe we can make you an offer."

"Why would you want so much land? Even if it's divided, it's not like you'll have them right on top of you." She didn't want to talk about Luke and definitely did not want to have to see him. The less she saw of any Hamilton, the better actually.

His gaze was so familiar as the hazel eyes met hers. "What happened with Luke the other night?"

"What? Nothing. We ate pizza, he dropped me off

and left." Annoyance was obvious as she answered. "Why?"

It was his turn to seem off put. "Just asking. He's gone to Billings for a few days. Hospital."

"What happened?" Her eyes rounded. "Did he do something?"

"No. Fuck, forget I said anything. He's gonna kill me."

"Where is he?"

AFTER TOBIAS LEFT, Leah wondered why she'd asked anything. Maybe it was a sign, his getting sick. Fate was telling her she wasn't ready for a relationship, and especially not with a guy who had more issues than she did.

Maybe he wasn't a cheater like her ex, but the demons that came back with him from the war were a foe she wasn't sure she wanted to fight against.

And yet he continued to fight. Had not only gone overseas, but also came back to continue his own war.

CHAPTER TWENTY-TWO

THE CLINIC WAS nicer than Leah expected. As she made her way down to Luke's room, it almost felt like someone's home. Most doors were closed but the ones that were open showed simple set ups with very clean line, Swedish type furnishings.

"Leah?" A woman she recognized as Luke's mother approached. "How are you?" The pretty woman hugged her and smiled. "You are so beautiful."

She'd run into the woman several times over the years and each time she said the same thing. Leah couldn't help but wonder if it was because she'd been such a plain teenager.

"Thank you Mrs. Hamilton. How are you?"

Luke's mother guided her to a sitting area, set up like someone's living room. "Good sweetheart. I'm so happy Luke finally agreed to come here. I've been pestering him for years. This clinic was set up by doctors who served over there. They came back and started this place to help soldiers dealing with the after effects of war time."

Leah looked around the serene space. "It's so peaceful here. I almost want to ask for a room."

Luke's mother's lips curved. "It is. Luke is doing well. He's been here only for a short while. Not really supposed to have too many visitors, so only I have come by and he kicked me out." She chuckled softly. "Says I am trying to baby him. I'm glad you came. I think you may be the reason he's finally agreed to seek help."

Her heart tumbled at the thought. "I'm not so sure. We don't exactly always get along that well." She looked toward an open door. "I probably shouldn't see him then."

"Nonsense. I'm sure he'll be glad to see you. I was just leaving." She stood and Leah did as well not sure what to do next. "See you soon dear." The woman gave her a quick hug before walking away, her sandals clip-clopping on the hardwood floor.

This was a stupid idea. She held a journal and pen, which now seemed like a stupid thing to bring. But she'd not wanted to show up empty handed and it was hard to figure out what to bring someone who was dealing with any kind of psychological issue.

"LUKE?"

Other than wearing sweats, he looked the same. Same handsome face, same air of badass and same flat eyes when meeting hers.

He didn't speak, nor did he invite her to sit. Instead

his gaze moved from her face to the items she held.

The long silence was awkward. Shit. She'd not been sure what to say to him and now that he didn't seem at all receptive to her being there, her mind went totally blank.

"I brought a journal and a pen. Thought it could be something you could use." She walked to a small table next to the bed and placed the things down.

He didn't look at the items she'd brought, instead turned to look out the window. "Why are you here?"

"I'm not sure. I suppose because I wanted to see you."

Ever so slowly he nodded, his wide chest expanding with each breath. "I'm good."

"Thought you could use some company." She neared, but stopped when his eyes snapped to her.

"I don't."

For a moment Leah wasn't sure how to react and she could only look at him. Eyes flat, he met her gaze for a moment before looking away to where she'd placed the journal and pen. "You can take that with you."

If he wanted to ensure she never spoke to him again, he was doing a bang up job. Why had she even tried?

Just because they'd had sex did not mean he felt anything for her. The notion that they'd connected on their last date had definitely been one-sided.

"Throw 'em in the trash if you don't want them," she finally said, unable to keep her voice down. "You're such an asshole."

She whirled on her heel and left the room, barely able to keep from cussing more.

Not bothering to speak to the nurse or attendant who sat at a desk in the entrance, Leah hurried past to the safety of her car.

Why had she come? He was there to get away and despite what his mother thought, the guy didn't want her anywhere near him.

"What an ass," Leah said out loud. "And I'm an idiot."

She drove to Billings to visit her mother, needing to forget she'd ever met Luke Hamilton.

A WEEK LATER, Mother Nature decided to give Montana one more blast of summer and Leah was glad for it. She opened the windows and doors allowing the house to warm up, not caring if it was a bit too hot.

When her cell dinged, she read the display and looked around the space before answering.

"We have an offer," the male real estate agent sounded giddy on her phone.

"For how much?"

"There was a bidding war. Ten thousand over asking price," the agent said. "When can we set up the closing? The buyers are anxious to move forward and want to set it up within thirty days."

The wind blew leaves in through the front door, they fluttered across the wide arches leading to the dining room, on past through the dining room. Leah followed the progress and they floated out the open French doors to the back yard where Rosie slept on the deck.

"Let me think about it. I will call you back on Monday." She hung up not giving the guy time to try to manipulate her to answer right away. That they'd accepted the asking price and offered ten thousand more shocked her. She'd priced high expecting lower offers.

Rosie walked through the door and scratched at the cabinet where her treats were kept. That particular one would need painting now.

Moments later, treat in her mouth, the happy dog scampered back out and she followed it outside.

It was a beautiful clear day, barely a cloud in the sky. In the distance she could make out Luke's red heifers. They'd taken to hanging out close to the property line, seeming to like the fresh grasses there and had become a constant reminder of him.

She blew out a breath. Accepting the offer meant she'd be able to return to Billings. Back to her condo, where she could prepare to return to work. Four long months remained on her sabbatical. Time was moving slowly and yet at the same time, once the property was sold, she'd only have ninety days remaining.

For some strange reason, the thought of returning to her corporate job at Morgan Investments didn't hold the allure it once had. The pang of missing it was gone now. Although she did look forward to the availability and convenience of life in the bigger city, she'd become accustomed to the slower life in Laurel Creek.

Should she sell the property? Maybe it was possible to remain and work from there. There were many opportunity's for consulting and such.

Leah considered what her father would say. He'd left the decision of what to do with the land up to her.

Just then the phone rang again and she was surprised to see it was her brother.

"Hi Matt," she said into the speaker. "Long time."

Her brother's deep voice was friendly. "Hey. Dad told me you're at the ranch. The family and I are coming up next week. The girls want to see you. Got room for a rowdy family?"

Her heart leaped at the thought. "Of course!"

They spoke for a few moments and she decided the timing was perfect. She'd put off setting a sale date until discussing everything with her brother.

Leah went back to the door to keep an eye on Rosie. How long had it been since she could spend time with her brother's family without it being squeezed in between long office hours or perhaps scant minutes on a Sunday?

He'd not said how long they were staying, but it occurred to her that it didn't matter. Not one bit. Her lips curved as she considered what she needed to purchase to prepare for her two young nieces.

"ANYBODY HOME?" ALLISON arrived later that day with her usual flurry. Windblown hair and a massive flower print bag on her shoulder, her friend smiled wide. "I brought wine!"

ALLISON SAT BACK lifting the glass of wine to her lips. "So much is going on. You've got my head spinning."

"Actually mine is too and it's not from the wine. I keep changing my mind. It's not like me at all. Once I make a decision, I stick to it. But this time, things are different. It's my family. My home."

"What did your dad say?"

Her father had not sounded happy, but he'd agreed about it being her decision. "He said the land was mine. That he didn't want me to feel I had to keep it just to make him happy."

Allison nodded, her lips curving. "What do you think Matt will say?"

"Matt and Cheryl love living on her family's land, so he'll probably try to talk me out of it. He's never been interested in working at the company. Loves the farm life."

More and more she could see why, as the night sounds wafted in through the open windows. There was little that could compete with the peacefulness of life there. "I can't believe I used to find being here so boring. Funny how being older changes one's perspective."

"I am considering moving to Laurel Creek."

Leah was surprised at her friend's admission. "Why? You don't have anyone here do you?"

"Nope," Allison replied. "After Mom and Dad passed, my brother and sister both moved away. They're both in Seattle and other than the rental house here, we don't have any roots. The lease is almost up and I am thinking it would be an awesome place to open a shop on the first floor and live above it."

"What about David?" Leah said, referring to Allison's boyfriend of almost ten years.

"David is David. He goes with the flow. I'm not sure he'll want to come with me."

Her friend's boyfriend was not who Leah pictured as the one for Allison. Although she didn't dislike the man as he'd always been nice and attentive to Allison, there never seemed to be a special spark between them.

"What if he doesn't want to come with you?"

Allison shrugged. "Then he won't. I'm not sure I want to continue the relationship anyway. We have been spending less and less time together lately. He's even hinted to moving out to Butte to be closer to where his kids live."

"Butte?"

"Yep." Allison shuddered. "I think my coming here would give him the excuse he needs."

"Wow." Leah leaned back wondering about all the changes. "So, when I go back home, you won't be in Billings for me to hound anymore if you move here."

"Unless you change your mind. Anything can still happen," Allison said in a singsong voice. "You never know. Mr. Prince in shining armor may be right around the corner."

"My last so called prince is in a mental hospital…and he kicked me out the one time I tried to visit him. His armor is rusty."

Allison giggled. "He's working the kinks out. He'll be back around. It was probably embarrassing for him. I mean what guy wants a girl to see him in a clinic. He probably wasn't sure how to deal with it."

"I don't think he's my prince either way."

"Right."

"What does that mean?"

"I mean, you care more than you want to admit."

"It was just a fling. I'm sure my heart will recover." Leah placed the back of her right hand over her forehead. "Some day my real prince will come."

Allison giggled. "Then again, we may be too old for princes. We need to settle for the clock maker or the baker."

They got up and took the dishes into the kitchen. Allison flipped on the television to a music only channel. "Let's sit on the porch for a bit. I want to look at the stars."

"I have a better idea." Leah hurried to the linen closet and dragged out an old comforter. "Let's lay on the grass while we do it."

Moments later they lay side-by-side, a content Rosie with them as they watched the starry sky.

"We used to do this all the time and plan our futures. Now we're both in our forties and it's here."

Leah laughed. "Yep. We didn't quite live up to our expectations did we?"

"Are you kidding me?" Allison turned to her with a wide grin. "We are kicking ass."

A falling star streaked across the sky and out of habit Leah made a wish. She certainly didn't feel as if she was kicking ass at the moment. If anything, life was having a hay day kicking hers.

MATT, HIS WIFE Cheryl, and the girls arrived late on Monday morning. Leah blinked back tears when both her nieces rushed to her with open arms. They'd grown so much since she'd last seen them only months earlier. She made a vow to herself in that moment as the giggling girls ran back to get their small bags. Never would she allow so much time to pass again between visits.

"Hi sis." Matt came toward her lugging a suitcase and a tote bag. Which being it was pink definitely did not belong to him.

She hurried to help him only to be engulfed in a tight hug.

"We have news," her brother announced, looking back at his wife.

CHAPTER TWENTY-THREE

L UKE BROUGHT HIS horse to a stop atop a small hill to take in the view. Although Taylor had assured him the cows he'd purchased were fine, he wanted to check for himself. The damn things had taken to hanging out near where the fence had been worked on, which meant they were out of sight from the house and stables.

Sure enough, they grazed lazily on tall grasses, not bothering to take notice of him.

In the distance, he made out Leah's black dog racing toward him. Tongue lolling out of its mouth, the dog barked protesting him being so near. Obviously, the animal had become territorial and protected its home.

Luke dismounted and walked to the fence. Upon seeing him crouch down, the dog hurried closer wagging its tail.

"So much for protection," Luke said reaching through the wide vertical posts to pet its head. "Hi Rosie. You're not supposed to wag your tail."

A whistle sounded and both he and the dog looked toward Leah's house. She stood in the back scanning the area with one hand shading her eyes. In a blue blouse and cut off shorts, she looked sexy. She looked towards where he and the dog were but didn't acknowledge him.

From so far away, she couldn't tell if it was he or Tobias. Luke lifted his hand in greeting.

Leah took a moment before responding with a slow wave of her hand, no doubt hoping it wasn't him.

"Go on girl. You're being summoned," he said to the dog that gave him one last look before scampering toward its owner.

Although he felt like shit over how he'd treated her, it was for the best. She didn't need someone like him in her life and the sooner he accepted the future would not include a woman, the better.

Luke mounted up and headed back to the house. His mind was constantly on Leah. Probably hated his guts and with good reason. He'd acted pretty badly when she'd gone out of her way to visit.

The journal she'd given him was safely tucked in his t-shirt drawer. He had plans for his next steps in setting down roots and starting his new chapter. It didn't include a woman. But damn if he didn't keep picturing a beautiful blonde every time he thought of what it would be like.

Making his way to the house from the stables, Luke chuckled as Speck, the tiny dog raced toward him. The little dog had adapted well to life there and it was comical to see how it commanded attention, and got it from all three of them.

"Hey Speck." Luke bent down to scoop the little dog up. It wiggled and licked his face before kicking its legs signaling wanting to be put down.

His phone chimed and Luke was surprised at the displayed name.

Christina Hamilton.

"Hello."

The last time he'd heard from his ex-wife had been almost two years earlier when she'd needed him to sign some paperwork so she could sell the car they'd owned together. Now her voice sounded breathless. Immediately he stopped walking and prepared for whatever news she'd give.

"I'm getting married. I wanted you to know."

He wasn't sure why she felt the need to inform him, except that she was a nice person. Christina had given him more chances than he'd deserved. Had been patient until he'd gotten so out of control. It had sucked when she'd asked for a divorce. But in her defense, between stints overseas, he'd frightened her with the severe flashbacks and refusing to seek treatment had not helped matters.

"Congratulations. Who's the lucky guy?"

There was a long silence and his gut tightened.

"Charles...Charles O'Brien."

Luke couldn't speak. How and when had she gotten to know him? Could it be the same person he thought?

"You mean O'Brien's father? The kid that I served with?"

There was throat clearing. "Yes. I met him at the funeral. You refused to go. We've kept in touch and then last year we began dating."

"Not sure what to say."

"I know. I don't expect you to say anything. It's just because of who he is that I wanted you to know from me. We're happy Luke. He's moved on and wants to start a life with me. I want you to be happy too. To hopefully fall in love, get remarried. You deserve it."

After she asked about his parents and that he'd give them her love, Christina ended the call.

If ever there was a twist, this was one he didn't expect. From what the kid had told him, O'Brien's parents were already divorced before he died. He tried to remember why he'd not gone to the funeral. It would have been the right thing to do. Guilt however had stopped him.

How many funerals had Christina attended in his place?

Letting out a breath, he looked up at the sky just a huge cloud moved across it. The formation blocked the sun for a few moments and then continued its trek. Life did go on it seemed.

It didn't matter whether a person enjoyed it or hated it.

Since his return to Laurel Creek, after spending two long weeks at the clinic, he'd been doing well dealing with things. He vowed to take each day as it came and not think too much more into the future than warranted. Now he wondered if perhaps what he'd done was allowed guilt to take away what could have been a good life.

All the years wasted, letting his mental issues overtake him. Letting the guilt stop him from living.

"MOVE YOUR SHIT out of my way." Taylor tried to maneuver around Luke's gym bag while carrying a wooden box into the living room.

"What the hell is that?" Luke followed his cousin, curious to what was in the dusty box he carried. "Where'd you drag it out from?"

"I found this in the garage. Looks like all kinds of old crap. I mean really old."

Taylor placed the box down with care. "Not sure why we hadn't noticed it before. I'm cleaning things out to put up shelves."

Two hours later, now joined with Tobias, the three sat in silence. In the box were old pictures of ancestors, some drawings from Tobias' namesake, and quite a few odds and ends of items owned by the Hamiltons back in the 1800's.

"I can't believe Mom and Dad never said anything about these. They should be better stored." Tobias held up a sketch. "I'm having these framed."

Although his brother was gifted, he'd not done any artwork in a long time. Luke met his gaze. "You should do more artwork."

His brother shrugged.

"What do you want?" Taylor picked up a horse that had been whittled by someone. "This is like a time capsule."

Looking over the items his ancestors once used, Luke's gaze kept going to a wooden box. "I want this." He picked it up and studied it. On the bottom the initials "E.J." were etched.

"We should ask your Dad what he wants to do with the rest," Taylor suggested, but none of them moved.

Tobias, always the more introspect let out a long breath. "They're gone, the people responsible for us being here. Ain't that strange that we hold items they once held?"

"Yep and here on the same lands," Luke said looking at the box. "It feels almost like an honor. We're lucky they were strong people who left us land and a way of life."

"Did you know Leah is selling her land? Some realtors were there the other day. Wonder if she's got some offers," Tobias told them.

"No shit? Damn," Taylor replied looking at Luke. "Did you know about it?"

"Yep."

Thunder sounded in the distance.

"Summer storm," Taylor mumbled, looking at him. "You gonna be okay?"

"I'm good." Luke looked out the window. "But it

may scare the horses."

"Thought of that," Tobias said. "Better close the stable doors."

All three got up and hurried out. Instead of walking, they got into a truck to get there faster.

Once they returned, the rain began falling.

"It's gonna be a gully washer," Taylor said shaking the rain off his hair while on the porch.

Tobias laughed. "Just because we were digging around old junk doesn't mean you can start talking like that." He turned to Luke. "Coming?"

From the truck Luke met his brother's gaze. "Nah. I have to check on someone."

CHAPTER TWENTY-FOUR

THUNDER SOUNDED ONCE again and she jumped. "I have to go." Leah's hand shook as she placed the cell phone on the couch arm. It had been a long time since she'd been so furious. Of all the things to do, this was the worst. The realtor had been shocked when she'd shouted at him and although she'd apologized before hanging up, she still felt bad for taking her anger out on the poor guy.

Coming there to the ranch and attempting to do anything was a huge mistake. Not only did she not follow through on her first idea of making it a cattle ranch, but now she was backing out of selling it. Especially not to the person who'd offered extra money.

"Anxious buyer my foot," Leah said stalking to the front door. She needed fresh air, to walk off the emotions that didn't make sense. Perhaps it was all the time alone that was affecting her. Although rain began falling, the wide front porch would be dry.

Or it could be her brother's announcement that they

were expecting a third child. Too much happened. Where was her life in all of it?

Someone knocked and she stomped to it. When she yanked the door open, the last person she needed to see stood on the porch drenched.

"You need to get the fuck away from me right now," Leah said pointing past Luke to his truck. "I am so over you."

His gazed moved over her and he frowned. "Can I talk to you?"

Past the point of reason, Leah's teeth chattered at the words. "No. I don't want to talk to you."

As if to accentuate her statement, lightening criss-crossed overhead and Leah took a step backward. "You'd better go."

Luke didn't move. Instead he let out a long breath and the muscle on the side of his jaw flexed. "I apologize."

Giving up and not wanting to be struck by lightening, she turned and went back inside flinging the door closed. Of course Luke blocked it with his foot and followed her in. On the verge of angry tears, she squeezed her eyes shut. This was not the time to cry, she was not going to act like a damn girl in front of him.

"What do you want Luke? To rub in my face that you're outbidding any other buyer for my land?"

"Why won't you sell it to me?" He was magnificent in a tight black t-shirt and black hat. A villain impossible to tame. "It's what you want isn't it? To leave, go back to your office job."

Office job? Did she even have that anymore? Her biggest client had asked for his account to be transferred to Zack. Apparently they'd hit it off over drinks.

Her dog, who had been hiding under a blanket since the storm started, rushed from under it to Luke, wagging her tail and acting as if Luke were there to save the day. The dog fell back allowing him to rub her belly when he bent down to greet her.

He straightened his face, hard to read as always. "I apologize for acting like I did when you came to see me. I was embarrassed."

His apology caught her off guard and she almost said the cursory "it's okay", but it wasn't "okay". He wouldn't get off that easy.

"You know what, whatever. I get it. Let's just leave it at that. I'm exhausted, not sure what the hell to say to you right now."

There was a long pause, then he took his hat off and held it down to his side. "It's hard to explain how much I've lost. The war took some of my friends and guys I was supposed to protect. I allowed it to take my marriage and time with my family I'll never get back."

He looked down at his boots. "I don't expect you to understand and it's not an excuse. I offered to buy the land so you can get it back if you ever change your mind."

Leah's mouth fell open. "What?"

When he lifted his gaze to her, she lost her breath at

the pain reflected. "I don't want you to lose the opportunity to pass this place and your family history to whoever comes after."

"I don't have children Luke. Like you, I allowed my work to take things. Too many things."

The right corner of his mouth lifted. Probably the closest she'd ever get to see him smile. "You might still."

"Ha. I'm in my forties."

His shrug almost made her smile. Her brother was in his forties, his wife as well. The pregnancy was a surprise, but they were happy. Perhaps it wasn't too late for her, but then again, unless she went to a sperm bank, it was so not happening.

Finally she relented and walked to the kitchen, knowing he'd follow. "I just turned down your offer. Told the realtor I'd changed my mind. I admit, the main reason was that I didn't want to sell to you. But another reason is that I am not sure I can go through with it."

He moved closer and pinned her with a darkened gaze. With her emotions all over the place, the last thing she needed was a fling with a guy that would leave right after.

"I don't want to lose any chance I have with you. Tell me what to do."

Okay so this was so not what she expected him to say. The day was supposed to end with her drinking wine while calming a nervous dog and crying into a half-gallon bucket of ice cream.

"What do you mean exactly?" She'd misunderstood

him before, so Luke had to explain what the hell he was talking about.

"Today I realized everyone moves on, even those who've lost so much more than me. I planned to stay here in Laurel Creek, start my own ranch, and fight daily to keep the monsters at bay. I planned to do it alone, so I wouldn't make someone else miserable when I have to be alone, or need a way to control my anger."

He reached for her hand and pulled her closer. Leah didn't resist, but she stopped short of any part of them touching. "Why are you telling me all this?"

"Because when the storm started, I hurried to ensure the horses would be safe, yet the only thing I kept thinking was that you were alone and that I didn't like it. I want to be sure you are safe. You matter to me. Tell me what to do. I want to be your man, Leah."

Once again she could only stare at him. Damn if the guy didn't just melt her heart. As much as she wanted to be strong, resistance flew out the window to join the storm in a dance.

"Stay the night. Keep me safe."

He tugged her to the couch and they sat down. When he opened his arms, she settled against his side. Luke placed his hat on the ottoman next to his outstretched leg.

"Tell me about the war."

There was a long silence and then he began talking.

"There was this kid named Keller O'Brien, the most optimistic person I've ever met. Even while under fire, the kid kept his cool and would rarely lose his temper...."

Leah listened to him talk about people that had probably died. His deep voice stable and strong as the storm raged outside. Rosie jumped on the couch and settled on the other side of Luke and promptly fell asleep.

While listening to him describe things she never imagined, her eyes became heavy and slumber claimed Leah.

CHAPTER TWENTY-FIVE

T HEY WALKED SIDE by side down the sidewalk after leaving Melba's diner. Luke attracted attention. His muscular body combined with height and good looks were a sight. He tugged her against him and kissed the side of her head.

Although he didn't talk a lot, the way he communicated with actions was more than enough.

Just as they stepped off the sidewalk to cross the road, a truck turned from the street directly toward them. The driver caught sight of them and slowed, but barely. The asshole continued moving forward expecting them to move out of his way.

Leah held her breath when Luke pushed her behind him, every muscle tensing.

Oh no. She took his hand and pulled him back. Jaw set he watched the truck driver who hesitated to get out of the truck upon taking in Luke's size and expression.

The dumbass climbed out acting as if he didn't see them.

"You almost hit us," Luke said, advancing toward the idiot who glanced to her then Luke.

"I didn't hit you. So that counts, right?" Okay so the asshole proved her assessment of him. He went to walk away but Luke stepped in his path. Finally it dawned on the genius that a huge muscle bound guy was pissed enough to punch his face in.

The guy lifted his hands. "Man, sorry. I didn't see you until I was almost parked. I should have stopped." He looked to Leah. "Sorry about that."

Leah held her breath as Luke's hands clenched into fists. The guy noticed it too and took a step back.

After a silent moment, Luke turned to her. "Let's go."

A long breath left her burning lungs and Luke gave her an understanding look, lips pressed together.

She reached over and tapped the end of his nose. "I love you."

His rounded eyes met hers. "You do?"

"Mmm hmmm."

They walked to her car and Leah could've sworn she saw him smile.

LUKE WAS COMING for dinner. He'd offered to cook, claiming to be tired of eating with his brother and cousin every night. She smiled since he'd been over at her house most evenings.

They'd yet to make love and although she understood he was trying to prove himself, a part of her missed
it. Although the times they'd made love it had been more
of a hook-up, it had still been amazing.

This night, she did not plan to give him the option
of leaving. Since the night of the storm, he'd yet to stay
over.

Rosie barked outside. Through the window the familiar blue truck approached and there were yaps as Luke
lowered Speck to the ground. The tiny dog raced around
in circles chased by a delighted Rosie.

Moments later, Luke walked in with two bags of
groceries. His gaze went straight to her. "Hi."

Leah laughed. "Hi yourself. What all do you have
there?"

AS DELICIOUS AS the steak dinner had been, Leah was
anxious to be with Luke, so she'd hurried through the
meal while assessing how best to move forward.

Luke helped her clean up and afterward poured two
glasses of wine.

"I'll be right back." Leah excused herself and went to
the bedroom. She removed her clothes and straightened
the lines of her panties. After that, she brushed her hair
out and applied lip-gloss.

Satisfied, she went to the dresser and lit two candles
she'd placed there earlier and turned down the blankets.

Her stomach flipped as she touched perfume to her

neck and down the center of her breasts.

"Luke, can you come here for a minute?" She waited by the bed, feeling sensual in the candlelight, lingerie and high heels.

He walked through the door with the wine glasses in hand and stopped, his gaze roaming over her then looking into her eyes. "Damn. Wow."

The statement made her lips curve. "Thought you'd like to help me finish getting undressed."

After placing the glasses on the dresser, he took in the candles for a moment. Leah was fascinated by the lowered brows and slight flare to his nostrils. Over the last few days, she'd learned to read him better. Although Luke was a master of masking how he felt, there were little tell signs.

"Definitely. Where should I start?" He reached for her bra strap, and slid it off her shoulder and pressed a kiss to where it had been. His mouth lingered on the spot and she cupped the side of his face.

Leah leaned her head to the right and closed her eyes as his tongue trailed up the side of her neck to her jaw and back down. His hands wrapped around her waist and he pulled her against him, the friction of his clothing against her bare skin sending shivers up Leah's spine.

"Oh," she exclaimed when he bent and took her exposed nipple into his mouth. Luke sucked it in hard and she gasped.

Nipping at the tender tip, he'd then pulled it back into his mouth each time ensuring to be gentle enough not to hurt her while his hands slid up and down her back.

The flicker of heat grew until burning and Leah pressed herself against Luke needing more. His mouth lingered over hers for a moment. "Don't move."

When he backed away, she missed his touch. The gratifying view of him undressing almost made up for the raw need that made her squirm.

First, he kicked off his boots and then his fingers curled under the bottom of his shirt. Inch-by-inch of his tanned flesh was exposed when he pulled the shirt up over his head exposing not only a perfect muscular physique, but also the scars on his left lower side that reminded her of his heroic past.

When he bent to push his pants down, his darkened gaze met hers and Leah licked her lips in anticipation.

Damn if the man wasn't spectacular. She could stare at his nude form for hours.

The thick rod between his legs caught her attention when he moved toward her, each fluid step with the grace of a dangerous yet beautiful predator.

When he towered over her standing so close, the heat of his body caressed her. Leah lifted her hands and cupped his jaw. "You are so attractive Luke."

His lips curved into a breathtaking smile. "Thanks." This time when his mouth covered hers, the ever elusive sense of hope beamed and Leah became lost in him.

Every touch and kiss that followed from his caresses to the way they took from each other became a discovery.

The flickering candlelight cast shadows over them, making the room almost magical.

A storm raged outside while in the confines of her bedroom walls, the lovers joined with a tempest of their own.

Leah cried out when Luke drove into her, his movements hastened by need. When she shattered, falling from the precipice, his hoarse call mingled with hers.

They made love again, only this time faster and harder, like a means to an end.

Neither wanting to be apart, they showered together, a sensual experience as they lathered each other's bodies.

It was the most wonderful night Leah could remember and as much as she wanted to know where things would go next, she dreaded the evening to end.

It shocked her when he slid between the sheets with her after discarding the towel he'd wrapped around his hips.

She snuggled against him and released a long breath. Words formed and were discarded as Leah tried to formulate how to ask him to stay the night.

"Care if I spend the night?"

Joy sprung and she lifted her eyes to him. "I want you to."

Within moments his soft snores sounded and Leah couldn't help but chuckle at how fast he fell asleep. Unlike him, she remained awake enjoying the feel of the large body against hers, the security of his heavy arms, and the hard chest beneath her cheek.

LEAH WOKE TO the sound of dogs barking and the smell of coffee. She sat up realizing Luke was not in bed. After pulling on an oversized t-shirt and underwear, she trudged to the front room. Through the window, she caught sight of Luke. He leaned on the front porch post with a cup of coffee in hand and watched Rosie and Speck as they raced about chasing each other.

"Good morning," she said walking out and wrapping her arms around his waist. "You're up early."

His gaze traveled over her face, the warmth in it taking her by surprise. "Figured Speck would need out. Didn't want him to have an accident." Luke pressed a kiss to her temple. "Got any breakfast food? I can make you something."

MOMENTS LATER, SHE sat at the table with a cup of coffee he'd insisted on making for her. Luke moved about the kitchen frying bacon and eggs as bread toasted. It seemed so odd for him to enjoy cooking. Although stoic and of few words, it seemed he was the type that showed affection by doing.

When she offered to help in any way, he would frown and shake his head. *Cute.*

The meal was delicious and after eating, she was finally allowed to help. They washed and dried the dishes and cleaned up the table and counters.

Leah let the dogs back out leaving the back door open and turned to Luke.

"I'm going to get dressed and then head to town. What are you doing today?"

He studied her. "Working at the ranch. Helping Taylor and Tobias."

Leah walked to the bedroom with Luke behind her. Needing to ensure they were still on the same page, she wanted to ask him so many questions, yet at the same time, it felt awkward still. So instead, she went to him and pulled him down for a kiss. Luke responded. He pulled her into a tight embrace, his mouth lingering over hers.

When he cupped her behind, his hardness pressed into her.

While kissing he guided her back to the bedroom where they made love. It was slow and gentle at first until they both needed to find release, then they raced to completion. Leah lay spent on the bed with Luke sprawled over her.

Once again, they showered together. It was nice to share the bathroom space as she brushed her wet hair and he brushed his teeth with a new toothbrush she gave him.

"Do you want to come over for dinner tonight?"

He met her gaze in the mirror. "Yes."

CHAPTER TWENTY-SIX

LUKE PULLED INTO a parking space and walked across the street to where Leah's friend Allison stood. He admired the pretty lady, her curls and long skirt blowing in the wind. With her hand shading her sparkling eyes, she smiled at him. "Hello there. How are ya?"

She looked across the street to an old house that he remembered always being there.

"Did Leah mention I was moving back to Laurel Creek?" Allison looked to him. "In a couple of weeks, I'll be here for good."

Their relationship was still new and they'd talked about this and that. Mostly getting to know each other. "Yes, she did."

"I'm turning my grandmother's house into a flower shop and living on the top floor." She motioned to the old house. "It's been painted and a small kitchen is in the building stages upstairs. Just waiting for contractors today to work on replacing the windows and for displays to be delivered."

Luke considered it strange that Leah had not mentioned her own future plans to him yet. Instead, she'd skirted the subject, other than mentioning she planned to keep the house and land after all.

"I remember your grandmother. She wasn't very nice."

Allison laughed. "Oh I know. That woman scared the crap out of me." The woman let out a sigh. "I hate that Leah is moving back to Billings just as I'm coming back."

The statement caught him off guard. Leah had not mentioned what would happen after the six month sabbatical was up. It was as if she didn't want to discuss it with him.

"Her sabbatical is almost up."

Unaware he didn't know Leah's specific plans, Allison nodded. "I know that, but I was hoping with her loving the ranch so much and then you and her...you know seeing each other, she'd change her mind about going back. She could do consulting and work from here."

He shrugged and hoped to look nonchalance. "See you around." Tightness around his chest made him ponder if perhaps instead of going to the hardware store he should get in his truck and hightail it back to the ranch before something happened. It had been a while since he'd had any kind of flashback or anxiety, but the familiar stirring left no doubt.

Instead of going to the store, he went to a bench

beside it and sat down. He took in long breaths and followed the visualization exercises Dr. Sullivan had given him. Luke repeated calming words in his mind until his breathing slowed and the tightness, although still there, loosened some.

HEADING BACK TO the ranch, he would have preferred to bypass his own and go to Leah's instead. But decided not to go there until taking time to think things through. Although Leah had professed loving him, they'd not made any plans for the future. Perhaps, she planned to return to her life in Billings and they'd have a long distance relationship.

There was also the possibility she did not want to stay with him. The thought hurt, but he pushed past it. Although he'd not told her yet, he loved the woman and had hoped for a permanent thing with her. Marriage even.

Every time he considered it, thought about his future there in Laurel Creek, it included Leah. But he'd not told her, had not asked, afraid it would be too soon.

And now she planned to leave.

To be fair, it was a lot to ask. He still had so much to work through. Although managed for now, there were no guarantees when it came to PTSD. Both he and Leah knew no matter how hard he worked at it, the shit could head south without any kind of notice.

"HEY MAN," TAYLOR called out when Luke began unloading feed and other supplies. His cousin joined him hauling a large sack over his shoulder. "Lots to do today. Hope you don't have plans until late."

"Nope. I'm here 'til we're done."

The day was full. Between cleaning the stables, working with the horses and restocking, Luke was glad he didn't have time to ponder the situation with Leah.

By the time they staggered back home that evening, the sun was setting and the prospect of showers and bed meant they gobbled up leftovers.

Luke showered and watched television in bed, barely able to keep his eyes open when his phone dinged. It was Leah.

He texted a short message letting her know he'd stay home that night. Not only was he too tired to go anywhere, but also the doctor had warned against doing something emotional when exhausted.

The sci-fi show on the television screen was a good escape and yet his mind kept returning to what Allison had said. Leah planned to leave soon. Why had she not told him?

Following a knock, Tobias poked his head in. "Hey you asleep?"

"Nope. What's up?"

His twin walked in and shoved his hands into the jeans he wore. A sure sign something bothered his brother. "I think I should go talk to Tori. Her mom got diagnosed with breast cancer."

Victoria McBride owned the pizza restaurant in town and was also Tobias' high school sweetheart. They were not anywhere close to on friendly terms.

"Not a good idea if you're only going to end up arguing with her. She doesn't need that right now."

"Yeah. I'm tired of avoiding that place. It's been over thirty years that we broke up, we should be able to get along without losing our tempers." Tobias sat on the bed and Luke moved his legs to give him space.

"Especially since both of you got married to other people after you broke up with her."

Tobias met his gaze. "I was gone, wanted her to move on... have a life." His brother let out a breath. "I made a big mistake marrying someone else. I know that now. I suck."

"No argument from me on that," Luke said with a chuckle. "Leah is leaving." He had to tell someone, bounce his thoughts off of and all that.

Tobias' eyebrows rose. "Really? That sucks."

"Yeah. I thought there was something between us... shit. But, what do I know?"

His brother bent his head in thought. "You need to ask her to stay. If you want her to stay, then ask her. Have you done that?"

"No."

"Why not?"

They both knew the answer. He was afraid of her reply. It wasn't fair to ask her to stay with him. His future wasn't exactly rosy. First of all his plans to start a ranch would mean long hours and with his issues, he'd have to take breaks and step back whenever it was required.

"Yeah all that, but still. If you love her and she you, then you'll make it work." His twin's lips twitched at having read his thoughts.

Luke scowled. "I hate when you do that."

"Yeah well, it's not like you don't do it to me."

True enough. Luke knew the underlying reason for Tobias' resentment toward Tori. He'd never stopped loving her and because of Victoria McBride, his twin brother was ruined for other women. Every single relationship since his relationship to Tori had ended disastrously. His brother had even married a great woman just to prove he was over her. It had not worked.

"Dude. Talk to Tori. Tell her you're sorry about her mother. Offer any kind of support we can give and then get away as fast as you can before you end up in an argument."

"Yeah, I might do that." Seeming satisfied with his advice, Tobias stood. "I'm crashing early. I'm beat."

"Me too."

"Hey."

"Yeah."

"I'm glad you came home."

Luke let out a breath. "Me too bro."

CHAPTER TWENTY-SEVEN

TWO DAYS SINCE she'd seen Luke. He'd not come by because of long work days at the ranch. Although Leah understood, she missed him and it hurt her feelings that when she'd offered to bring dinner over he'd declined.

That they weren't sure what time they'd be done was a feeble excuse in her opinion. Of course, her thoughts kept revolving around the fact that perhaps he was backing away from her.

A relationship was so much work. The second-guessing and doubts plagued constantly. She'd wanted to discuss her upcoming final decision as to whether or not to move back to Billings. Her father had relented and offered she return sooner. A part of her had been so relieved that she'd agreed right away. But after telling Allison and hearing it out loud, she'd wondered if it was really what she wanted.

A long distance relationship with Luke could work. Billings wasn't so far that she couldn't be there every weekend. Or if she had too much to do, he could possibly travel there. Were they even at that point yet?

There were the factors of who would take care of the house and the land, plus now that she'd decided to keep it, what to do as far as ranching or farming.

She poured hot water into the tea dispenser and waited for the leaves to steep while keeping a watchful eye on Rosie who seemed to be chasing something into some bushes.

After a few moments, she went to the door and called the dog back.

Rosie hurried toward her, her snout dirty and tail wagging. Leah couldn't help but wonder if her dog would miss having roaming freedom.

With a happy bark, Rosie raced toward the front door leaving a path of dirt and leaves.

Leah opened the door and went to the front porch as Luke's truck neared. He brought it to a stop and his gaze met hers.

The first time she'd met him, he'd been so intimidating. The mental picture formed of the frightening large muscular man stepping out of his truck to talk to her about the fence.

Now once again her heart quickened as he climbed out of the truck.

In a black t-shirt, jeans and boots, he looked every bit the Montana cowboy he was. "Hey," Luke called out before going to the back door of the truck.

He bent to retrieve something and she caught a

glimpse of his well-formed rear.

When Luke straightened with a large bouquet of flowers, her breath caught. There was vulnerability in his eyes, his eyebrows flat and jaw set, as he walked toward her.

"Being I'm about to ask for a lot. I wanted to bring you these."

She accepted his kiss and studied him. "Sounds serious." Leah took the flower vase and sniffed them. "They are beautiful. Where on earth did you get them?"

"A new flower shop in town is about to open. The lady helped me. She said these were your favorite."

Allison was very well aware she had a weakness for lilies.

After placing the flowers in the center of the table, Leah waited for Luke who scratched Rosie's stomach.

When he straightened, he took her hand and led her to sit on the couch and lowered next to her. "I guess I may as well just say this."

Her stomach tightened at his serious expression. "Whatever it is, spit it out. You're about to make me throw up."

"Will you please stay here? In Laurel Creek. With me?"

"Oh my God." Leah threw her arms around his neck and hugged Luke as tears threatened.

His arms encircled her. In his arms, she found the security she'd yearned for. Luke gave her strength and only with him did everything fall into place.

When he pulled back, she kissed his lips and sighed. "I wanted to talk to you. I needed to know where I stood. It was hard to make a decision about whether to leave or stay based on our relationship because it's so new."

She couldn't stop talking. "I want to stay, but didn't want to pressure you, so I had pretty much decided we could try long distance."

"Oh hell no." Of course his face remained serious and she met his gaze. Luke shook his head. "If you want to move back to Billings, I'll go with you. I can find a job or something."

"You would do that for me?" Leah couldn't believe that Luke cared enough to give up his plans and follow her. He'd yet to declare how he felt, but from his actions and words at the moment, he showed her more than words ever could.

His wide shoulders lifted and lowered. "I would do that for you, yes."

"I'm so confused." Leah closed her eyes. "What do you think?"

They talked for several hours weighing the pros and cons of every alternative. Leah was astonished at how articulate Luke was. She discovered one of his jobs in the Army was project management. He was not only well rounded when it came to planning, but also fair and impartial. He never goaded her decision process by sharing what he planned.

She knew he wanted to settle in Laurel Creek and

that the open spaces, small population and slower lifestyle were better suited for his PTSD. Yet he didn't bring it up, insisting she concentrate on what she wanted out of her career.

Finally, after scanning the long lists and crumpled papers they'd written on, Leah sat back with a wide grin. Luke looked from her to the papers in front of her.

"I've made a decision," Leah declared. "It's what makes the most sense and what I keep coming back to. The three most important things in my life right now." She counted off on her fingers. "You, this ranch, and Rosie. I suppose I should also say Allison." Leah began laughing. "Please don't tell Allison I picked Rosie over her."

The look on Luke's face was priceless. He blinked rapidly and she could have sworn his eyes were shiny with tears. He stood and rounded the table.

When his heavy arms enveloped her, Leah leaned back. "I want to stay here with you. I love my life and can't imagine living anywhere else."

They made coffee and walked out back to ensure the dogs didn't get into mischief.

"This is wonderful isn't it?" A peace fell over Leah and immediately she knew the right decision had been made.

Luke put his cup down and moved closer. Taking the cup from her hands, he then tipped her face up and kissed her. The kiss was soft yet not without demand. It was gentle, while at the same time conveying emotion.

"Thank you."

"For?" She caressed his jaw. "What are you thanking me for Luke?"

"For loving me back."

She pretended to be shocked. "Did you just admit to loving me?"

Instead of a reply, his mouth covered hers. Luke would prove exactly how he felt by showing her. As she gave in to his kiss, the dogs rushed inside. They probably didn't want to be left outside as the couple would no doubt head to the bedroom to not emerge until morning.

"Smart dogs," Luke said as he lifted her into his arms and headed inside.

CHAPTER TWENTY-EIGHT

A LLISON HUMMED AS she painted the antique dresser she would turn into a display for jewelry and ceramic boxes for trinkets. The soft music wafting through the room and aroma of freshly baked shortbread made for a perfect afternoon.

She and Leah were to spend the next day at the ranch perusing catalogs and choosing items to order for Allison's inventory. She'd bring shortcake and spiced tea.

Her new shop, Enchanted Woods, would open in a couple of weeks. Already she did brisk business selling flowers from the front room. It seemed the residents of Laurel Creek were excited about a gift and flower shop.

Not for the first time, Allison stopped working to look out the wide front window. She and her boyfriend of almost ten years had split. It had hurt to see the look of relief when she'd informed him she planned to move. At the same time, Allison had been aware things were not going well between them.

So many decisions had been made in her life based

on what others wanted. This time she was doing something because it was exactly what she'd dreamed of doing for years. To run a beautiful little shop in a small town. A place she could live out her days and not worry about whether or not someone else agreed with whatever she did.

There was another strong reason for her decision. She held her breath as a person who sparked more than her interest walked up the steps and onto the front porch.

He scowled at the wreath on the door before pulling it open.

Allison straightened as he walked in.

"Good afternoon. I was told you could help me with flowers?" Taylor seemed uncomfortable.

Allison's stomach lurched at being alone with Taylor Hamilton, the man she'd often daydreamed about.

"Sure, how about you look over those." She pointed to a small cooled display. "I have three to choose from, all of them are very pretty."

He glanced at the flowers giving her a chance to study his handsome face. "I need them delivered. To someone in another town."

"Oh." Allison became curious. "I can certainly help you chose something, you'll have to use FTD delivery. To whom are we sending these to?"

"Janice Hamilton, my ex-wife."

She hesitated, fingers over the keyboard of her laptop. "Of course."

Allison couldn't believe her luck. The man was still

hung up on his ex.

So much for expecting something to happen between her and Taylor.

More to come… Read Broken: Taylor
coming this winter

Whether a rancher, a highlander or a hunky cowboy, you will fall in love with Hildie McQueen's heroes!

Dear Reader,

I hope you enjoyed Jaded: Luke. I have first hand experience to the changes that serving during wartime can cause. My husband and coworkers were all deployed to Afghanistan and Iraq when the war broke out. Two have since died returning, one took his life. The sacrifice of the brave soldiers, airmen, sailors, marines and civilians who serve sometimes continues after long they return.

If you are looking forward to Broken: Taylor, to be released this winter. I can't wait to share his story with you!

Ex-detective Taylor Hamilton is broken. After the devastating loss of his children and parents, his marriage crumbled and fell apart. No matter how easygoing he appears, sadness overtakes him when he's alone. His way of dealing with it has him headed straight for disaster.

Allison had two reasons for returning to her childhood home of Billings, Montana: a fresh start after a failing relationship and a handsome rancher she's loved since high school. When Taylor thwarts her plans by courting his ex-wife, her heart is crushed once again. Perhaps there is a way to get his attention, even if it's not entirely honest.

Do Taylor and Allison have a second chance at love, or will they destroy each other in the process?

I love hearing from my readers and am always excited when you join my newsletter to keep abreast of new releases and other things happening in my world. You can also follow me on Facebook and Instagram.

Newsletter sign up:
http://goo.gl/PH6D00

Facebook:
facebook.com/AuthorHildieMcQueen

Instagram:
instagram.com/hildiemcqueenwriter

Email:
Hildie@HildieMcQueen.com

Website:
www.HildieMcQueen.com